I0726928

The Pumpkin King and Other Tales of Terror

THE PUMPKIN KING

and other tales of terror

R. DAVID FULCHER

GRAVELIGHT PRESS | LOS ANGELES

**THE PUMPKIN KING
AND OTHER TALES OF TERROR**
(being a collection of short, ghastly fiction)

ISBN: 978-1-957224-06-0

gravelightpress.com

DEDICATION

To my wife Lisa, for her love and support,
and my brother Dale, for his guidance on this manuscript
and in all things fantasy and science fiction.

ALSO BY R. DAVID FULCHER

<u>FICTION</u>

Trains to Nowhere and Other Stories of World War II

Blood Spiders and Dark Moon, Tales of Horror,
Science Fiction and Fantasy

The Cemetery of Hearts, More Stories of Horror,
Fantasy and Science Fiction

The Lighthouse at Montauk Point and Other Stories

<u>NONFICTION</u>

The Movies That Make You Scream!

CONTENTS

The Pumpkin King and Other Tales of Terror

Eulogy to E.A. Poe

MAN OF dark musings and opiate visions!

Mind of pits and rats,
Black cats and ancestral corpses!

How is it that love sparkled within those dark recesses,
Like diamonds within a bedrock of obsidian—
That verse sprang from that ebony hand,
As vibrant and unlikely as lilacs from snow?

Tales of cities under the sea,
Of waves weeping softly, "Annabel Lee!"

Did the bells, the bells, the bells, foretell of your demise,
Or was it borne on Raven's wings, thus falling from the sky?

Could it be that your last vision was your brightest?

Oh, soul of all that is night,
Inspire my pen to wail and to write.

Marienburg Castle

AT FIRST, they were mere specks in the sky. The specks became white wedges, like falling pieces of crème pie. Closer still, they appeared as marionettes, dancing with umbrellas across the horizon. Finally, when they were very near the earth, one could see that they were paratroopers.

Walker was first to touch ground; the pilot stumbled in a half-fall on the field. Goldstein, the radio operator, tumbled to the earth a close second. Wilkins, the navigator; Croft, the bombardier, and Earl, the ball turret gunner followed Goldstein. They did not wait for Floyd, the copilot, or the others to descend.

There would be no miracles; the others were dead.

Walker took the lead and the crew fell in behind him across the fields which skirted the blackened, levelled village. The glare of the afternoon sun made him feel exposed and vulnerable.

"Get down," he urged, and the crew hunched low in the wheat as they crept toward the distant hills. A few defiant building frames still stood in the town, their stones the color of obsidian, their residents merely ashes and carrion in the streets. Everything retained the silence after the storm; everything retained the silence of the dead.

Except for the wind. It crooned and sang sweetly while sifting the ashes of its beloved, laid cool, dew-laden hands upon the corpses which bloated in the late summer sun.

Walker and the others paralleled the country lane which led upward into the hills. They were edgy. Every movement in the distant tree line became the positioning of enemy troops; every obscurity a machine-gun nest or artillery emplacement.

They were edgy and they were on fire. The heat was unbearable.

It bore down on them and pressed their heavy flight jackets against their uniforms until both garments became a single, heavy, extra layer of sweat-laden skin.

Walker brought the company to a halt by a small stream. "Every man get a drink and cool down. I'll watch the hills. Earl, you watch the town. The first two to finish come and relieve us."

Walker withdrew his government issue .45 from the leather holster and wiped his brow. He'd lost his pilot's cap while bailing out. Too damn hot for it, anyway. Earl crawled on his belly up to a small rise behind their position and took up his watch on the village.

Where are they? wondered Walker. American airmen are a valuable prize for the Nazis. *Is it possible that no one on the ground saw us going down? Is it possible that the German fighter pilots did not radio us in?*

No, he concluded, *it isn't possible. When a bird like the Fortress goes down it's no secret. It can't be.*

Deep in contemplation, Walker continued to scan the hills. Suddenly, he noticed a break in the tree line, an irregularity which was higher than any tree jutting skyward.

"Psst, Earl. Come over here," he whispered.

Earl scrambled across the ground on his belly and joined Walker. "What's up, Chief?"

"Look at the hills out there. Do you see anything peculiar?"

"Naw, just a bunch of trees. No—wait a minute. I see it. Looks like a tower, though it's too far away to be sure."

"That's what I think, too. If it's a tower I'd like to reach it before nightfall. Round up the men. Tell them we're moving out."

Earl nodded and crawled over to the stream.

Walker looked at the distant hills once again, and at the sun which had mercifully begun its descent toward night.

Once within the cover of the trees, they were able to move quickly. They reached the keep at twilight. *Marienburg* was carved over the arched entrance to the courtyard. An old, tattered swastika fluttered in the breeze next to an ancient coat of arms.

Walker took the swastika in his hand. "Cute," he muttered, and tore it off the wall. "Ready?" he asked the men.

"Yeah, right," muttered Wilkins. Some of the others laughed until Walker motioned them to silence. He tapped his holster. Those who had sidearms drew them.

They entered the courtyard. The castle sprawled out in the distance, a giant hexagon with towers at each junction where the sides met. A cathedral rose high above it all, its single spire expanding up into the sky and dwarfing the surrounding forest.

The entrance to the central part of the keep was barred by an inner wall and a large wooden door.

A sign on the door read: *Vorsicht! Hunden!*

"Wilkins, you can read a bit of Kraut, can't you?"

"Yeah. It says: 'Beware of dogs.'"

Walker rapped on the door with the butt of his pistol. There was no reply.

"Maybe they're sleeping," muttered Croft.

Walker looked puzzled. The wind rose up and swirling dust devils of dead leaves formed in the courtyard. *"Sssssstorm,"* it seemed to whisper. Darkness was beginning to fall, and the fat shape of the moon hovered on the horizon.

"We should get inside," urged Goldstein.

"Scared of the dark, Jew Boy?" cajoled Croft.

Walker turned and scolded his subordinate. "Shut up, Croft! We got enough problems without your mouth!"

Croft turned red with rage and stomped off into the courtyard.

"Let's open it," commanded Walker, ignoring Croft's display. They pushed against the door, but it would not yield. "Ready? Again! 1…2…3—PUSH!" Again, the door would not budge.

Finally, on the third try, the wood groaned and split, and the squad spilled inside. The cathedral hovered directly before them, its stained-glass windows shining like jewels in the moonlight. The castle stood adjacent to the church, silent and dark, sealed behind thick iron doors and high barred windows. They ascended a stairway onto the battlements and stared out into the night-enshrouded valley.

"Holy Jesus!" muttered Walker. The woods surrounding the keep were filled with small pinpoints of light.

"Fireflies," Wilkins said, "I guess Jerry's got 'em here just like we do back in the States. Sort of reminds you of home, huh?"

"Did any of you get the feeling we were being watched on the way up? I could swear I saw something trailing us," Earl said, his voice dropping off to a whisper.

"You've also seen Jerry fighters that weren't there, Earl," laughed Wilkins. "Sometimes you even take a damn pot shot at 'em!"

The crew's laughter eased the tension, and the men began removing their flight jackets for comfort.

The wind spoke again, this time more pronounced than before: *"Volkssssturm,"* it hissed.

"What did that sound like to you guys?" asked Wilkins.

"The wind. Just the wind," replied Walker, stretching.

"No. It was a word. *Storm* something," said Goldstein. "I don't like this. I'm going down to the cathedral." Goldstein stood up and descended the stairs.

Then Wilkins rose.

"Don't tell me you got cold feet, too!" exclaimed Walker.

"I can't look out there any longer," said Wilkins, motioning out beyond the battlements and into the onyx night.

"Those things…fireflies, whatever—they're getting closer, I'm sure of it."

"Suit yourself," said Walker, "just watch out for Croft. He's madder than a hornet and spoiling for a fight." Wilkins nodded and left.

He's shivering, Walker thought.

Taking advantage of the quiet and the space, Walker balled up his flight jacket and stretched out on the battlements. The distant mantra of crickets lulled him into sleep. He dreamt of flying a Fortress into the sun.

—

Walker awoke abruptly to a scream. He rubbed his eyes and stared down into the courtyard below. The courtyard overflowed with eyes, some belonging to bloated, burnt corpses, and others to hollow, skeletal sockets.

To the left of the courtyard, he saw Goldstein. Freshly impaled on a stake, Goldstein screamed like one of the damned. Walker sucked in his breath at the sight, and in so doing, drew the attention of a thousand eyes. They could taste the blood that thundered in his veins. They could taste it and thought it delicious.

The seething mass moved toward the battlements, wielding pitchforks, clubs, axes, and rifles. Some wore swastika armbands and carried submachine guns.

Walker backed up toward the edge of the wall, an errant foot knocking his .45 into the endless drop beyond. The *Volkssturm*—the people's militia, a national army that would fight to the death and, if necessary, beyond death itself—surged up the stairs to meet him.

The Pumpkin King

One two-three-four-five-six.
One-two-three-four-five-six.

My lungs were burning in the cold autumn air, and sweat traced an icicle down my spine. I've heard people say they enjoy running, but I've never believed them.

It's sheer hell—but a hell I am willing to endure to retain some semblance of physical fitness. To distract myself from my air-deprived lungs, I glanced at the quaint homes aligning the street, yards decorated by dry, multi-colored leaves that emitted the sound of bones scraping together whenever they reached concrete or asphalt.

There were also jack-o'-lanterns. All kinds of jack-o'-lantern; round, tall, big, small—each hand-carved gourd leered at me with misshapen, toothy grins. Accusingly. They were right to be upset.

Because this year my front doorstep was without a jack-o'-lantern. Chalk it up to a lack of holiday spirit. Still, I felt a slight twinge of regret as I jogged past each one, wondering if it wasn't too late to make amends. After all, tomorrow was Halloween.

A knot suddenly grew in my side that made me forget about Halloween, jack-o'-lanterns, and almost everything else. It was a side stitch, a detestable discomfort that caused pain with every breath. Fortunately, I was close to home. I increased my pace, breathing deeply through my nose and ignoring the protests of my leg muscles. *One-two-three-four-five-six.* Finally, I reached the streetlight I used to mark my finish and the agony began to subside.

I bent over to regain my breath, feeling foolish for working my body beyond its abilities. If I kept this up, I'd likely be dead in a ditch by age thirty-five. I removed my Baltimore Ravens cap from my head and ran my hand through the remnants of my thinning, sweaty hair. I continued walking, passing my Belmont Square townhouse and cooling down. My thoughts returned to Halloween. I wondered why some went all out with decorations while others ignored it. Correction: While people like *me* ignored it. It was easy enough to blame my religious upbringing. Devout Christians never seemed fully comfortable with this odd pagan holiday.

I climbed the few stairs that led up to my townhouse, unlocked the door, and stepped inside. The place felt so empty since my roommate moved out. I quickly locked the door and switched on the television to chase away any malicious shadows.

After a quick shower, I threw on clean sweats and was soon back downstairs. Famished, I began removing a pot and boxed pasta from the cabinet when I heard a sound that caused my blood to freeze and the small hairs on the back of my neck to prickle up.

Thump-thump.

It was still light outside. Silly to be scared. Most likely someone was at the door. But few things annoyed me more than being disturbed after a workout, particularly by a salesperson.

Annoyed, I whipped open the front door. The grinning faces of the jack-o'-lanterns across the street greeted me. A moment later, I noticed something at my feet. Kneeling down, I found myself examining a small jack-o'-lantern, done plainly with triangles for eyes and nose, and one square tooth in its nondescript mouth. I quizzically scanned the street in both directions, looking for whomever had "gifted" me the item, but I saw nothing and heard only the breeze whipsawing through the adjacent woods.

I placed the jack-o'-lantern on the top step. Perhaps whoever had left it had done me a favor after all. I shut the door. As I walked back to the kitchen, there was another knock at the door.

Vaulting across the carpet, I ripped open the door, and jumped onto the landing where I nearly tripped down the front steps. The streetlights were now on, making it even easier to confirm that I was alone in the October twilight. I thought I felt something brush against the legs of my sweats, a slithering sensation that cats sometimes give you when they wrap around your ankles. Looking down and seeing nothing, I closed the door behind me and turned the deadbolt.

Hopefully the pranksters were tiring of this game as me.

I began to walk through the living room back to the kitchen but suddenly stopped dead in my tracks. There, atop the coffee table, rested the jack-o'-lantern, its insides aglow with an unholy light. I stood frozen for several moments before willing myself to approach it. Finally, I gathered the courage to move closer for inspection. The light inside the jack-o'-lantern exposed its interior, and whoever had carved it had done a masterful job of removing the stringy strands of pulp that usually clung to the squash's interior. What perplexed and terrified me was that the unholy reddish-orange glow wasn't the result of a candle or light bulb. It emanated from the very rind of the plant itself.

It was then that the pumpkin spoke to me.

"Cat got your tongue?" it asked slyly, its voice high-pitched and playful, like that of a jester.

"Who are you?" I stammered.

"Your worst nightmare," it replied.

I spun around and made for the door, half convinced I was hallucinating if not dreaming. I unlatched the deadbolt, but it clicked back into place as soon as I started to turn the doorknob. I turned back to the jack-o'-lantern.

"An easy trick, but effective," the jack-o'-lantern said, its orange light flashing in time to the latch on the deadbolt that it clicked back and forth at will.

"What do you want?" I begged.

"I want you to think on this. There is but one expectation of you this time of year. One simple obligation: To carve pumpkins. To pay homage to the king."

"What king?"

"Samhain, the King of the Dead." Its demeanor began to change. Its voice deepened and the reddish-orange glow rose like an enraged fire.

"This is ridiculous!" Now I was beginning to lose my fear and was feeling pissed. This thing, whatever it was, was in my house. I turned to climb the stairs and snag a baseball bat so that I could smash the talkative piece of vegetation into a hundred juicy bits. I was an educated man, and I knew of the myth of Samhain, the Lord of the Dead who arrived every fall to put nature in balance with the deadly strokes of his sickle. I also knew it was pure bunk.

I had only reached the first step when I heard a sound far worse than the maddening click-clacking of the door latch: the metallic whisper of a kitchen knife being drawn from the butcher block.

I turned back to the pumpkin. "Okay. You've got my attention. What do you want?"

"I want to carve you," it replied simply.

—

Belmont Square was peaceful at midnight on the night before Halloween. Children slept soundly, dreaming of ghosts, witches, goblins, and bags of candy, their slumber only occasionally disturbed by the sound of dry leaves that dragged across the street like the nails of a corpse. Pumpkins flickered and winked at one another, silently critiquing the newest display—a hollow human head, stained garish orange with pumpkin endocarp, and lit by a strange candle that flickered inside of it.

Heavenly Strains

TO HELL with God!" fumed Victor, as he stood in the church. Blue-black bags hung under tear-stained eyes.

Life had been fine. Not beautiful, not margaritas on a tropical beach, but fine all the same. Then Dad had to up and die.

"Damn him!" Victor cursed under his breath.

He clutched the top of a nearby pew, feeling awkward and alienated but most of all *alone*. The casket loomed ahead of him at the end of the aisle like a judgmental monolith, wood-brown for stilled blood and thick with death's certainty. He wanted to be a man before his father. He did not want to weep. Reluctantly, Victor took one step forward and then another. He moved as if he were someone else, a stranger in his own body watching himself on film.

Victor intensely wanted God to exist at this exact moment. He wanted Dad to be eternal, a minor angel in the constellation of the heavenly host.

And yet he raged against the Lord as well, boiled to get his hands around the neck of this soul reaper that pompously plucked people from the mortal sphere. Mothers from sons. Daughters. *Fathers.*

Victor was almost to the casket now. He steadied himself once again, as if the coffin emanated a veil of cold air that only the dead could pierce.

"Dad," Victor moaned, and fell to his knees, yielding up the last pretenses of hardness and allowing the tears to flow. There had been a hundred kindnesses, a hundred laughs, a hundred admonishments, a hundred shouting matches, and now—stillness. Victor was thirty and alone in the world, and the tears he cried were for himself as well, for the knowledge that at times like these pieces of you fall away leaving holes in the spirit. And he felt full of holes as he cried in this holy place.

Victor felt a hand on his shoulder. Perhaps it had been there for some time, like a leaf or a butterfly on your sleeve that never fully asserts its presence. And yet, as the sobs subsided, the hand remained.

Victor turned. A short man in a button-down shirt and jeans smiled down at him. "I know," he said simply.

"How could you possibly?" Victor hissed, pushing the hand harshly from his shoulder. It seemed disrespectful to be speaking with this stranger in Dad's presence.

"Your grief," the stranger continued, unfazed by Victor's hostility. "I know of it. I am the keeper of such things."

"How did you get in here?" Victor demanded.

Don't worry, Dad, I'll get rid of him, just like I used to get rid of those pesky salespeople for you and Mom when I was a kid. But those days are gone, right, Dad?

Right, son. Gone forever, son.

"I work here," the stranger replied, dangling a set of keys in his left hand. "I'm the organist." The man's tiny head and large ears reminded Victor of an evil gnome.

"I'd prefer to be alone. Church is on Sunday," Victor said, trying to suppress a growing anger.

"Oh, well," the organist replied, chuckling. "I don't play for any congregation. I play for folks like *him*," he said, motioning toward the coffin. "I play for the dead. Calms them on their journey and all of that."

"I don't know what kind of sick freak you are, but you'll be playing for yourself in a minute if you don't go away."

The organist shook his head, chuckling. "I know," he said. "Your anger. I know of this, too."

Victor lunged out to grab the annoying man by the collar, but only reached thin air.

Once again, he felt a hand upon his shoulder.

"Your rage. I know."

Spinning around, Victor shot forward and was sent sprawling through space toward the floor, hitting his head on the pew and sending Bibles and hymnals flying.

Victor roared and rose. The organist was nowhere to be found. The church was empty. Muted sunlight fell through the stained-glass windows as incense wafted through the slow air.

There was an agonizing creak of a hinge as the lid of the casket slowly began to open. The organist suddenly appeared from behind the coffin and stared at Victor without humor. "Your fear," he intoned deeply. "I know."

The organist disappeared and the lid came crashing down. There was a moment of stillness as the flickering candles in the church debated the virtues of incandescence. Suddenly, Victor covered his ears as the metal diapasons erupted with an explosive sound that sent a tingle through the spines of the wooden pews. The sensation ran all the way up Victor's arm. The dark, somber music reminded Victor of the dirges intoned by Captain Nemo during his lonely voyages under the Seven Seas.

Slowly, the lid of the coffin began to rise once more. Victor collapsed atop the casket, desperately attempting to wrap his arms around it to force it shut.

The tempo of the music began to increase.

"You can't control it, Victor," a voice boomed over the frenzied stanzas. "You can't control the dance of the bones."

The music grew to a fevered, harmonic pitch, and the wood of the coffin lid blew apart. Chunky splinters pricked deeply into Victor's face and arms as a cold hand clasped Victor's wrist. He looked down in horror. His father's eyelids suddenly opened, revealing two obsidian orbs, as he lay in the remains of the wrecked casket.

"Dance with me, son." He looked at Victor with calmness and love.

An icy chill raced through Victor's arms and flooded his chest. It stopped his heart cold. The church began to spin, a miasma of candles, stained glass, and the mad chorus of a mad organist who now stood as he pounded out the notes of his woeful dirge.

"I know of your death, Victor!" the organist screamed as he played, grinning madly.

"I know," Victor replied, and slipped away.

A Matter of Taste

MARY MCKELDIN sat in the hospital room watching the green waves of the EEG attached to her young son rise and fall. Tears had smeared her mascara, leaving black lines which radiated outward from sunken eyes. Mary's small hands were white at the knuckles where she clutched a purse and handkerchief. The pristine room seemed cold to her, antiseptic. She decided she was glad that she had brought the flowers for Stephen.

The door opened, and Stephen's doctor entered. Mary stood up anxiously.

"Hello, Ms. McKeldin. I didn't realize you were here." Doctor Thomas removed his reading glasses from the breast pocket of his white jacket and examined Stephen's chart.

"Doctor, is there any change?" asked Mary breathlessly.

"I'm sorry Ms. McKeldin. Comas aren't predictable. Stephen could be in this condition for weeks."

"Or years?" asked Mary, her voice sharp and hostile.

The doctor set down the chart and frowned. "Yes, or years. He's breathing on his own, which is a good sign. Perhaps you should go home and rest for a while. There's nothing you can do for Stephen at this moment, and you'll be notified the moment his condition changes."

Mary nodded and walked over to her son's bedside. His small chest rose and fell, the only sign of life. Mary ruffled his brown hair and kissed his forehead, "Sweet dreams, champ."

Mary turned and exited the room quickly. Doctor Thomas stood and frowned.

—

Mary had a dream that night. It began in the hospital room. Doctor Thomas was examining Stephen, oblivious to Mary's presence.

Suddenly, the line on the EEG went flat, and a low electronic tone filled the air. The doctor looked up and shook his head sadly. He covered Stephen's face with the sheet. The area of the sheet over Stephen's mouth rose and fell softly.

"No!" shrieked Mary, "He's still alive!" She struggled to reach Stephen but found herself restrained. Following a moment of darkness, Mary found herself in a vast cemetery.

A funeral party had gathered by a fresh grave, and in the distance the pallbearers approached carrying a small coffin. Their white coats a stark contrast to the gray sky.

As they drew closer, Mary realized with horror that the pallbearers were doctors from the hospital. Again, she tried to reach her son, who slept soundly in his wooden vessel, but she once again found movement difficult, as if walking underwater. The pallbearers laid the coffin down by the grave, and Doctor Thomas opened the upper panel of the cabinet, revealing Stephen's angelic, upraised head. The doctors bowed their heads, and Doctor Thomas, who had removed a small Bible from his coat, began the sermon.

Mary saw Stephen's face in detail, as if watching from a zoom lens. The color on his cheeks seemed brighter against the white plush of the coffin's interior. His hazel eyes were open, but vacant, glassy, and unblinking. His nostrils flared softly and then narrowed again as he breathed.

The panel was closed. Mary hovered once again in darkness, and then another face began to form in the inky void, its features sharp and unfamiliar.

"Mary," it whispered, its eyes pulsing in the darkness like embers, "Mary, let me help you." The voice was dark and alluring.

For a second the features fell into focus—a large, trident-shaped nose; slender, pointed ears; and two small horns the color of fire. Mary recognized the visage with a chill. It was the face of the Devil.

Mary awoke suddenly. She was drenched in sweat, and her hands clutched the damp sheets and had pulled them into disarray. The clock on the nightstand read 12:01 in large red digits.

Mary's heart began to return to its even rhythm as she studied the familiar surroundings of her bedroom, but her mind remained in turmoil over what she was about to do.

She inhaled deeply and then spoke: "I invoke thee, Devil."

Nothing happened.

Mary racked her brain, then spoke again: "I invoke thee, Satan."

There was a sound like water being poured over hot coals, and then Mary gasped, for the Devil was now in the room with her.

Satan stood in the corner of the room, broad, muscular, and imposing, his body the color of molten lava. Although he had no visible sex organ, Mary felt irresistibly drawn to him, and her nipples stood out beneath the thin fabric of her nightgown. She immediately became red with embarrassment.

"Do not be ashamed, Ms. McKeldin. You are not the first person who has been attracted by sin, nor are you the first to call for my assistance."

The Devil paused, then looked at Mary. "What do you require of me?"

"I want my son back. His name is Stephen. He's in a coma," replied Mary.

"Let me begin, Ms. McKeldin, by saying that I can aid your son and bring him out of this condition." Mary's eyes shone with hope. "However, like any service, it requires payment."

Mary swallowed hard. "Do-Do you want my soul?"

"Certainly not, Ms. McKeldin," the Devil smirked. "I have more souls within my realm than I know what to do with. I require payment in currency."

"Currency?"

"Yes. Do not act so surprised. Germany has its Euro, England has its pound sterling. It is simply a matter of locale. Did I mention that you have lovely eyes?"

"No. Th-Thank you," stammered Mary.

"Which brings me back to my main point. The unit of currency in Hell is the eye, or perhaps more precisely, the eyeball."

"The eyeball?"

"Yes, they are quite a delicacy and exceptionally difficult to obtain in Hell, I'm afraid to say. I will return your son's health for the price of two eyeballs. But, at the time they are plucked—or shall we say, selected— the eyes must be full of sin. Sin gives them a certain sweetness, you see."

"Dear God," whispered Mary.

The Devil hissed and shrank back from this utterance, his long tail whipping about and throwing sparks.

"Be warned, Mary McKeldin. If you cannot pay the price, I shall take my services elsewhere."

"No! I mean, I can do it. I can get you your … payment."

"Excellent!" exclaimed the Devil, clapping his large, steamy hands together. "See that it is done. Invoke me once again when you have my payment. In the meantime, I shall see to your son. Good evening, Ms.

McKeldin." The Devil bowed low, then vanished with a puff of smoke.

Mary watched as a small red card drifted through the air before landing on the carpet. She rose from the bed and retrieved it. It burned her hand, and she quickly dropped the card onto the night table and switched on the lamp. She read it over and over again, trying to shake her disbelief:

SATAN'S SERVICES

"I'll do just about anything but windows!"

Eyeballs only, checks not accepted.

FAX: 666-6666   *Ask for me by name.*

"Dear God," whispered Mary again.

Then she went into the kitchen for a shot of brandy.

—

Mary checked herself in the rearview mirror. She thought she looked foolish wearing the black beret and sunglasses, foolish but definitely unrecognizable.

She had parked her car a block away from her ex-husband's luxury apartment complex. As she stepped out of her vehicle and started walking, the hammer in the pocket of Mary's trench coat pulled at her like an accusation. She had followed Frank, her ex-husband, and his secretary, a twenty-something bimbo named Charlotte, home from the office. Mary knew they would be in the middle of their quickie power lunch when she arrived. *So much the better*, Mary thought.

The day was sunny and brisk, and Mary drew little attention as she made her way to the complex. With every step, Mary contemplated turning back, but then she recalled how Frank had abandoned Stephen and her after the accident, and she knew she could do what she must be done to pay the Devil's price.

She reached Frank's tall, modernistic apartment building and withdrew the access card Frank had given her "in case something ever came up." She passed the card through the electronic reader on the door. It buzzed her in, and Mary continued through the lobby. The desk clerk was busy giving a tenant his messages and paid no attention to Mary.

Moments later, Mary turned the corner and ducked into a stairwell. She removed the hammer and the ski mask from the pockets of her coat. She donned the mask and bundled up the beret, sunglasses, and long coat, placing the bundle under the stairs. Her gloved hand gripped the handle of the hammer firmly as she began her ascent to the fifth floor.

Adrenaline coursed through Mary's body, and by the time she had reached the landing of the fourth floor she felt as if her lungs would burst. Finally, she reached the fifth floor. She leaned against the railing to catch her breath as sweat pooled on her forehead. Mary removed her apartment key from her jeans and opened the door just a crack to assess the hallway. It was deserted.

She crept quickly to Frank's unit and silently let herself in. She could hear Frank and Charlotte going at it in the bedroom, and she grew furious. Mary waited until she could bear the sound of their lust no longer. She entered the bedroom.

Frank was on top of Charlotte, grinning wolfishly.

Charlotte lay spread-eagle on the bed, eyes temporarily closed in ecstasy. Mary stepped up behind Frank and raised the hammer.

At that moment, Charlotte opened her eyes, and her mouth formed a wide oval of horror. Unaware of his impending fate, Frank kept going at it, grinning like a madman.

The hammer blow was strong, swift, and on target. Frank's skull cracked open with a sound that resembled splintering wood. He died smiling.

Charlotte began to shriek. Mary pushed Frank's body aside and covered her mouth.

"Quiet, you little bitch!" spat Mary, raising the hammer. Charlotte fell silent. Mary tied Charlotte's hands behind her back with stockings, stuffed a dirty sock into her mouth, and locked her in the bathroom, naked and convulsing.

Mary rolled Frank's body over on its back. Thin streams of blood crawled across the neck. She removed a small buck knife from her pocket and a photograph of Stephen taken before the accident. The boy's soft, brown eyes steeled Mary's nerves for the task ahead.

Mary unfolded the blade and got to work.

—

When she arrived home, Mary had a message on her answering machine. Frank's eyes, more precious to Mary than gold, were wrapped up in her handkerchief and securely tucked away in her purse.

Mary pressed PLAY on the answering machine: "Hello, Ms. McKeldin. This is Doctor Thomas. I wanted to be the first one to tell you that Stephen is awake and no longer comatose. Of course, he will have to remain here for several days under observation, but the possibility of a relapse is very remote. Please come to the hospital at your earliest convenience."

Warm tears coursed down Mary's face as she replayed the message to convince herself it was real. She collapsed onto the sofa and wept for a long time, until tears would come no more.

Then she remembered the price.

Mary stood up and removed the moist, bloodied handkerchief from her purse. She had a glass of wine and immediately felt its effects. Mary decided to summon the old boy then and there.

"Satan, I invoke thee."

At first it seemed as if the invocation had failed. Then Mary heard the familiar hiss, like bacon frying on a skillet, and knew that the Devil was nearby.

She determined that the sound was originating from the basement. Mary switched on the light at the head of the stairs, but the steps remained drenched in darkness. *Probably burnt out*, she thought, and began to descend.

After several minutes Mary was quite sure that she was no longer on her stairway, nor any one stairway, for the steps switched between stone, wood, and earth frequently. Things were dim and uncertain, and only an occasional torch illumined the way down.

The sizzling sound grew louder with every step. The wine was still very much in Mary's head, and she thought to herself as she giggled and almost toppled down the steps, *I'm on the highway to Hell.*

Mary reached a great oak door. It gave easily as she pushed it inward, squeaking on its hinges and rolling back to reveal the vistas of the damned.

She stood on a rocky cliff overlooking a vast sea of lava. Small islands dotted its surface upon which were built the conical huts of Hell's citizenry. Dim shades fluttered to and fro between their portals. A large black mass hovered on the horizon, and jagged bolts of lightning ripped open the charcoal sky, giving the whole place a strobe light effect.

Something moved quickly over the sea, bright red like a fiery comet. As it drew closer, Mary recognized the speeding form as the Dark Angel himself.

The Devil drifted close and hovered before Mary, large and vital, teeming with the energies of his chaotic plane. Mary felt a resurgence of the animalistic lust she had experienced in her bedroom, and she grew warm between her legs. Embarrassed once again, she turned her attention to removing Frank's eyes from the handkerchief. They fell into her palm, smooth and slimy, and she offered them up to the Devil in supplication.

"Excellent, Ms. McKeldin, excellent! However, I regret to inform you that, due to inflation, my fee has increased to four eyeballs."

Mary was struck dumb with horror, and she turned to run. The stairway had vanished, replaced by tumultuous plains of liquid fire.

"You would prefer young Stephen experience a relapse?"

Mary sighed and shook her head as tears welled in her eyes. "Why my eyes, especially?"

The Devil grinned, amused by Mary's naiveite. "I requested eyes of sin. Murder, you must realize, is the sweetest sin a pair of eyes could witness. And my, how sweet your eyes must be, so chock full of murder and sin!"

The Devil raised the iron tool in his right hand.

Mary had mistaken it for a scepter, but now realized with an inward shudder that it was a pair of tongs forged in iron, black and smoldering.

Mary sat down on the stone and removed the photograph of Stephen from her pocket, desperate to burn the memory of his face inside her forever.

The Devil advanced, and Mary McKeldin paid his price.

My Days With Mahalia

The following writings were discovered in the footlocker of Second Lieutenant Stephen Davis. Officer Davis and his crew members disappeared along with their plane, the Black Mahalia, on June 14, 1944.

I AM writing this so that *she* will be remembered. Remembered not as a plane, for the Mahalia was much more than that (although her insides met the Boeing B-17G specs perfectly), but as a lady—one of darkness and passion that had every one of us flyboys who flew with her vying for her favor.

The most obvious feature that distinguished Mahalia from the other Flying Forts was her color—gleaming jet black; a stone spat out of a tar pit. Every other Fort I had ever seen had been delivered with the original factory chrome. That's how our co-pilot, Brian Briggs, thought up the name, Mahalia. Said the Fort reminded him of the fierce Hindu goddess of time, doomsday, and death. Kali, the black goddess. Briggs was always reading strange books. He thought Black Mahalia sounded dark and exotic, and somehow (although it made the more puritanical among us uneasy) it felt appropriate, destined.

Like I said, the color was the first thing we noticed as our squadron watched that graceful beauty touch down on the airstrip as if her rugged gears were ballet slippers. Up close, it was a different story. Up close we felt the overpowering feel of *her*, a fierce energy that engulfed all in her proximity with a hungry intensity, her need to feel the wind beneath her wings and fire on her skin. The first day she touched down we were hers completely, without compromise.

Flying raids—any kind of raids, whether over Central Europe, North Africa, or the Aleutians—are risky. First you have to get airborne. You gun the lumbering, four-engine beast across a narrow runway, all the while praying as it creaks and groans that just this one last time the rivets will hold, and the overloaded crate will take flight. Then things are OK. At least for a while. At 10,000 feet, you and your crew don oxygen masks and confirm that your flight suits are properly plugged into the electrical system.

There's no such thing as an airtight B-17. The cold hits you from everywhere. Your pale fingers pry at electronic switches with a minus-twenty-degrees touch and hope no one's suit goes dead.

Then, of course, there's flak and the enemy fighters. Flak fills the sky with dense, black clouds and continuous thunder. All of a sudden, an anti-aircraft ground gunner scores a hit. You watch through the canopy a plane in your formation loses a chunk of wing or has one of its radial engines ripped to shreds. The second-worst part is knowing you have friends in there. The worst part is knowing there's absolutely nothing you can do to save them. The flak is a hell that can be visited again and again. Believe it or not, you get used to it.

The fighters, however, you never get used to. The AA gunners 20,000 feet below are only distant shapes when you're in the sky. The fighters are much shrewder. In a single precision attack, they can annihilate your engines and watch as you begin the slow, fatal roll toward the earth.

I'm a ball turret gunner, and any crew member will tell you it's the worst position on the Fort. You fold your body down and into a Plexiglas bubble on the plane's underbelly and wait there, cramped and claustrophobic, as the world flows by beneath you.

But I'm rambling—let me get back to the Mahalia, which is the reason I'm writing this. The point I'm trying to make is that with everything that could go wrong on a flight, you get used to feeling a sort of nauseating uncertainty as soon as you climb into the bomber. I never met a guy who looked forward to a raid. Some put on good macho acts, but as soon as the bird began taxiing down the runway and shaking all over, their eyes revealed the truth: They were scared shitless.

When we were assigned Mahalia, everything changed. Our eyes beamed with bloodlust during the briefings, and all the talk of top-cover escort and secondary targets was ignored as we listened to the dark, imminent call of Mahalia as she waited in the wings. I sometimes imagined a voice in my head; Mahalia's voice: "Fly with me . . . we will drop black seeds and fire blossoms . . . we will burn, maim, kill, destroy . . . until death do us part."

Mahalia knew how to take care of her boys. Never once did an engine overheat, a machine gun jam, or a flight suit die. We scored direct hits on our targets and landed more kills than any other crew in the unit, indicated by the countless German crosses that covered Mahalia's nose. We were a squadron of average men turned legends, and for a while we were content not to question.

One day, following another particularly successful mission, our tail gunner—a youngster named Billy Webb—voiced our lingering doubts and broke the sacred silence of the topic like a shroud. He confided to me in the barracks late that evening. Beyond our window, but clearly visible, Mahalia waited in the field. Her aluminum fuselage bore a supernatural glow against slivers of moonlight.

"Steve?" he asked, trembling and standing wide awake next to my bunk.

"What is it, Webb? I'm trying to sleep."

"We need to talk about Mahalia."

"If there's something wrong, tell it to the mechanics. Let me be, will ya?"

Billy paused as a wind swept across the base and rattled the windows. I could sense him looking out at Mahalia with unease.

"That's just it. There's *never* anything wrong with her. And it's more than that. We never look at each other after missions. It's like there's a truth we all know but are afraid to admit. As if it's Mahalia up there doing the work, and we . . . well, we're just along for the ride."

I glowered at Billy, inwardly enraged that I couldn't face the truth of his claims.

"Listen, Billy, I'm not going to let you take away our accomplishments. We've worked our butts off to become a cracker-jack unit. It's that simple. If you can't handle it, then quit!" I engulfed my body in the supposed safety of my blankets and rolled away from Billy and the window. He said nothing, but continued to pace heavily by the window.

I closed my ears and drifted off to sleep.

—

I may never know why she abandoned us. Perhaps she needed a vacation, some time away from the children who lived and breathed within her steely bosom.

It really didn't matter why. She was gone, and for one of our hottest raids yet we flew not Mahalia, but just her shell—a standard B-17G that also happened to be painted black.

The mission was almost over before it began. During takeoff, the outboard engine on the left wing failed, causing enough drag that our wingtip nearly hit the runway before Captain Freeman could compensate.

At 200 feet, just as Freeman was turning back to abort the mission, the failed engine sputtered back to life. It was our first mechanical difficulty since flying Mahalia; we were shocked into silence. For long moments the buzz of the engines and the shrieking of the wind filled our minds.

We crossed the English Channel safely, but over the coast of France a portion of our vertical stabilizer extension was destroyed by flak. We felt even more morbid, which threw Freeman into a rage. A seemingly endless stream of obscenities raced from the cockpit across the intercom system.

Despite the tremendous psychological impact of the hit, the damage was technically minor. We were able to maintain formation and continue to our target in the heart of occupied France. Flying at an altitude of 30,000 feet, we drifted in threes, the cloud cover mercifully covering the ravaged landscape below. I daydreamed in my turret, feeling tired and nauseous and wanting to lay my soul down atop the carpet of white nimbostratus clouds beneath me and float forever. Suddenly I noticed three specks on the horizon at six o'clock, low and rising fast. I clicked on the intercom.

"This is Davis. We got bandits at six o'clock."

"This is Webb. I see it, but I don't believe it. Those aren't regular fighters."

The bandits closed in at an unbelievable speed. I swung the twin .50 caliber guns around and drew the planes into my sights. The guns felt cold and unresponsive in my hands. With Mahalia, they always felt like an extension of myself. Now they were foreign to me.

RAT-A-TAT-TAT! RAT-A-TAT-TAT!

The bandits moved too quickly, at least twice normal speed, and I couldn't compensate. They streaked up toward the tail out of my reach, leaving black trails of smoke in their wake.

"Jesus!" Webb cried. "They've got no props!"

RAT-A-TAT-TAT! RAT-A-TAT-TAT!

"Scratch one bogey at six o'clock," I said.

RAT-A-TAT-TAT! RAT-A-TAT-TAT!

"Damn! Missed those bastard Krauts," Marlowe, our left waist gunner called out. "I think they're the new Messerschmitt Comets. I heard the top brass talking about them, but I never thought I'd see one."

RAT-A-TAT-TAT! RAT-A-TAT-TAT!

"Damn! Damn!"

"Steve!" Webb called. "Two coming your way!"

I spun in the power turret and followed the black trails as the rocket-driven craft sliced the sky beneath me. I judged their speed and led the sights accordingly while I sat and waited.

RAT-A-TAT—click-click-click!

"Shit! I've got a jam!"

"Steve, what the hell is going on?" Webb cried.

RAT-A-TAT-TAT!

"I—"

"Shit, Webb's hit!" Marlowe cried.

I unplugged my flight suit slid out from the ball turret. The plane was shaking badly, and hundreds of empty shell casings rolled across the deck floor, making it difficult to walk. I steadied myself between the two waist gunners, Marlowe and Jones, their M2 Brownings spitting out casings in an endless stream, guns hot and teeth clenched. I stumbled back into the tail section.

The wind howled demonically at minus twenty and sucked me back to Webb. The tail turret was almost completely gutted. The fifties hung from the turret heavy and dead. Webb had been thrown backward several feet. Blood erupted from his right leg, which ended at the knee, and numerous shell fragments had cut him severely. A forehead gash fed the crimson stream. I held him dearly, primally, as an animal holds its young. Steam rose from his hot blood and commingled with the contrails that flowed out behind us.

Despite the chaos, we dropped our bombs on target. We cleaned up Webb as best as we could and left him in the freezing tail section. Our left outboard engine cut out again as we approached the landing strip. Freeman ordered everyone into the radio compartment. We averted our eyes from one another and spoke little.

In an attempt to avoid stalling, Freeman overshot the runway. The counterfeit Mahalia came down in dust.

Thus the betrayed, and the betrayers, ended their day.

—

June 14, 1944. A strange, relentless thirst has awakened me in the pre-dawn hours. I need to quench it. The small work lights are spread out over the darkened field like stars, and the moon hangs overhead like a god's lantern.

"Come to me . . . ," she whispers, that timeless woman I shall always love, my unquenchable thirst. "Embrace the night!"

I hear the lull of her engines on the breeze, soft like a perfume. She waits in the distance for her children. Slowly, one by one, we come to her, pale and uncertain. Webb is paler than the rest of us. He reeks of death and decay, but he, too, is reclaimed as her own. War is hell. Within that hell it does not bode well to betray those who love us, those who protect us from harm.

In my mind I answer her. *Worry not, lover. Fear not, ancient one. Be not afraid, Mama. I'm coming home to you.*

I know you will not understand, but like the others, I must answer. I must return to her. May all who read this forgive me.

To God and Country,

Stephen Davis
Second Lieutenant, USAF

A Night Out With Mr. Bones

I CAN'T *believe that Mr. Bones has done it again,* I thought to myself as I looked down at the coed, her neck awkwardly askew in the dirt. I was really angry this time. The girl couldn't have been more than twenty, but Mr. Bones didn't care about that. He didn't care about endless nights out partying with your sorority sisters, or making the cheerleading squad, or working hard at college to make your dad proud.

He just understood the killing part of it.

And once again he had left me here to do the clean-up.

The girl was fit and only weighed, at most, one-hundred pounds. It was easy for me to carry her warm corpse to the remote parking lot that backed up against the woods. The night was humid and still, and I sweated into my Oxford shirt as I waited at the tree line for any signs of activity. It was late, I was guessing around 2:00 A.M. With the exception of my Volvo station wagon some ten feet from my location, the lot was deserted.

I slung the girl over my shoulder and quickly fished out my keys. At a fast walk I reached the passenger door, flipped forward the bucket seat, and slid the body onto the back seat. I wished that I had a blanket or other covering, but if I had a blanket every time Mr. Bones came out to play, I'd need to upgrade my Volvo to a minivan in order to fit them all.

I walked around to the other side of the car and stepped inside. The car wouldn't start. The alternator protested in a whinnying shriek and the engine refused to turn over. *Damn you, Mr. Bones! What am I to do out here stranded in Parking Lot K with a dead girl in the back seat? How would I explain this? I could lose my tenure over this one.*

I waited a minute and retried the ignition. The engine caught, and I was soon winding through the pleasant, wooded lanes of the campus. I tried to lose myself in the peaceful surroundings, and slid Mozart into the

CD player.

Randomly, I shot a glance in the rearview and my blood ran cold: Mr. Bones was calmly staring back at me, humming along to the classical strains, hands folded neatly on his lap.

I scowled back at him disapprovingly. "Why?" was all I could manage.

"You know why. Just because. Because I'm me," he replied.

"Well, I'm out of it. I can't be shoveling shallow graves all over campus just because you lack self-control."

"You need me," he said sternly, quarry eyes shining out from the surrounding bleached whiteness of the skull.

"Bullshit. I need to teach; I need to get a mistress. At forty, I don't need this shit."

He just shrugged and looked out the window in an infinitely annoying way that resembled a petulant ten-year-old.

For several moments we were equally content to listen as the wind streamed past the car and watch the quaint, darkened storefronts on Main Street.

I don't like confrontation by nature, but I couldn't let this go.

"You could at least not sit on her," I replied with disgust.

"What does she care now?" he replied sardonically.

I guided the car on to the small, one-lane road that ran down to the river.

"When will you grow up and stop carrying on like this?" I asked.

"Parenthood is a bitch, ain't it?" he shot back.

There's just no talking to Bones when he's in this state. Funny, he's exactly what my ex-wife accused me of being—a poor listener who was unresponsive to emotional concerns. But this was a more serious than an extramarital affair, and as I turned my head briefly to the back seat the supple, limp arm dangling over the floorboards confirmed as much.

Enough was enough already. I pulled the car over onto the shoulder.

"What are you doing?" Bones asked. I smiled inside; he sounded genuinely worried.

"I'm not going anywhere until you can talk seriously about this."

"Vernon, this is not smart. We have to get rid of this dead weight before her smell seeps into this Yuppie ride of yours."

I waited a moment. Mr. Bones' neck joints creaked as he craned his head behind us to survey the road.

"The cops could come along any minute."

"I don't care! I want to know why you do it!" I was incensed, and no matter the consequence, I had to know if I would ever be free from Mr. Bones.

"Fine," he replied, teeth nervously chattering. "Then will you start the car up again?"

"Scout's honor."

To say that his expression was dead would be redundant.

"I know you think I'm evil," he began. I continued to glare at him from the rearview mirror. "But I'm not. There are others like me, others tasked with snuffing out life when possible. All over the world. Evil has patterns, distributions, all sorts of mathematics and ratios that have global implications. It's like the ecosystem," he replied cheerfully, hoping to sell his explanation to me by associating it with my love of nature.

I knew how manipulative he could be and let the comment just slide off. "Spare me the elevator pitch and cut to the chase." I noticed that the dead girl's head had shifted. I couldn't get the impression out of my mind that she, too, was listening to Mr. Bones. She reminded me of someone . . . a student from one of my lectures? Yes, was it Tiffany . . . no, Vicky! Vicky Strathmore, Anthropology 101.

Damn you, Mr. Bones,
Your death-head rattle
Strikes close to home.

"Okay, let's assume there *is* a Mr. Bones in Thailand—which there is, just as there's one in Singapore, Malaysia, and everywhere else in the world. Let's assume Thailand's Mr. Bones has just witnessed the building of a new hospital in Bangkok. Suddenly, there is too much good in the world—the Yin and Yang, the balance—such as it is—has lost equilibrium. Well, he gets on the horn and phones me, or anyone else in a different region, to perform some grisly act to counterbalance the goodness. We all work for the same God; we just do the dirty work. The work no one else is willing to do."

"So I guess you expect me to believe that you're the next pope?"

"Uh, can we get it moving, Vernie? I think I just saw headlights approaching."

"One more question," I demanded. Now Mr. Bones really did look anxious. He tapped his fingers against the dead girl's thigh to keep his cool. "If you get these 'assignments' as you say, how come you always go after women?"

"We're all allowed some latitude in the way we handle it. It's in the job description. The girls, the *women* as you say—that's just my thing.

I guess you could say it makes me feel alive, Vernie. Chock full of life."

Women chock full of life."

"Nice," I replied.

"Works for me. What do you say we resume our journey, Vernie?"

I grunted, and we got underway once again. There isn't much to say about the rest of the night that distinguishes it from the others. At least Mr. Bones helped with the digging this time. Needless to say, Vicky rests now by the riverside, alongside a hundred other girls in the rich silt. Several years ago I abandoned trying to give a decent burial service for them and just began tossing them in. Someday, one-hundred shiny sorority pins will rise up on one-hundred bony breastplates. I hope I'm long gone by then.

When I got home I was beat. I used Lysol on the car seat before walking inside. I tried to tip-toe into the room, but she always hears me.

"Vernon? What on earth have you been doing so late?"

"A few drinks with some of the faculty members."

I quickly walked into the bathroom to toss my muddied clothes in the hamper and run a hot shower. I always feel dirty after a night on the town with Mr. Bones.

Twenty minutes later I emerged in fresh pajamas, feeling human and somewhat aroused by my wife's slender form beneath the sheets. "Honey?" I asked.

"Oh, Vernie. It's late."

"Please?"

She turned to me, her brown eyes soft and absorbing and her voice soothing as silk: "Try to make it quick, okay?"

"That shouldn't be a problem," I replied, and we both laughed.

But it wasn't quick. It was long. And although I felt shameful, it was long because I was preoccupied by that damned Mr. Bones and the havoc he had caused once again. Finally, the release came, and I crumpled on to the mattress.

"Not bad," Vanessa cooed, and lay her head against my shoulder. Her body was sweaty. Her pulse raced. "Do you know why I love it?" she asked.

I barely heard her and muttered a noncommittal reply.

She continued. "I guess you could say it makes me feel alive, Vernie. Chock full of life."

My eyes shot open and I muffled a scream into the mattress.

"Excuse me, I have to use the bathroom," I said, pulling away from her.

"What's wrong?"

"Nothing. It's a guy thing," I said with a forced laugh.

My head swam dizzily from the draining events of the day. I leaned against the wall for balance and let my body slide down until I was sitting on the cold tile. I wrapped my arms around my knees and began to rock back and forth, "Not Vanessa. Not my girl," I kept repeating.

But then he was in the bathroom with me, as silent and sure as rainfall, his face reflecting off of the mirror like a cheap Halloween mask.

He didn't speak. I knew the challenge had been thrown down, the scales tipped in the favor of life and they—Mr. Bones, and the rest— would do the clean-up.

> *Mr. Bones*
> *Won't let me sleep*
> *The lives he takes*
> *Aren't mine to keep.*
> *The river is full*
> *The blood runs dry*
> *When spring rains come*
> *They'll find my lies.*

Merry Are We of the Lake

KEITH PULLED his collar closer, shielding the back of his neck from the cold drizzle. Red and green lights chased one another around the frames and sidewalks of the large homes that sprawled across the Hallowell community. All was silent except for the rain, which hit the pavement like the footfalls of cats.

Christmas trees silvered by icicles and gilded by ornaments floated behind large bay windows, close enough to touch but shielded by expensive security systems. Christmas Eve in the suburbs, Keith recalled, had the power to make people disappear—into churches, across state lines to the homes of distant family members, into joy, excess, and despair.

A couple emerged from a house on the opposite side of Rockaway Street. The woman wore a mink and the husband, looking somewhat inadequate in a wool sport coat, carried a bottle wrapped in a bow. They cast a disapproving glance in Keith's direction and then quickly exited in a brunet Cadillac Escalade.

Keith was a trim, bearded man of thirty-five. He wore a dark turtleneck, a North Face Gore-Tex ski jacket, and faded blue jeans. His slightly muddy work boots detracted from an otherwise clean-cut image. He cursed the rain for dampening his clothes while simultaneously cursing himself for caring.

He recalled another Hallowell of days past, one that had existed before the Yuppie invasion and the developers who transformed the simple Maryland dirt into gold. It had been known as Lake Hallowell, after the large lake at the west end of the community. The commercial district, such as it was, consisted of a Bob's Big Boy, a general store, a pump station, and a movie theater. Simpler times.

Keith knew they were watching him. He did not need to observe the sway of their brightly colored curtains to know that his passage had disturbed the children's dreams of Barbie dolls and Tonka trucks floating in the surreal darkness, eyes pulsating red and green. He was the antithesis of Santa, his soul an empty sleigh hungering the renewing joy and laughter of youth. They sensed his emptiness even on this night of selfishness and wished to gift him with … something, the wish manifesting itself by the pressing of young, pale faces against the windowpanes as Keith passed by.

Tomorrow, among the discarded giftwrap and bows, one house would be adorned with a body bag. Perhaps it would be the mother or father of the very children whose eyes now shadowed Keith. He tried not to think about it, and the persistent chill in the air was at least useful for forgetting.

Keith finally reached the jogging path along Old Baltimore Road that led down to the lake. The night was cloudy, hiding the moon and stars overhead, but he navigated the familiar path with ease.

The creek's black water murmured softly beneath its thin skin of ice, as if pleased to be able to speak without the summertime intrusions of frogs and crickets. A surge of adrenaline flowed into Keith as he spied the twenty-seven figures at the south bend of the lake standing side by side with their hands entwined. It always seemed to catch him off guard, but he couldn't imagine why—he had attended The Renewal for as long as he could remember. As he drew closer, Keith began to recognize the shadowy figures. Some had exchanged ponytails for bald spots, others bare fingers for wedding bands. But to Keith, they would always be the old gang of Hallowell High, the old murderous bunch that collectively killed on Christmas Eve.

Keith nodded greetings and acknowledgments as he walked to the left end of the line. He spotted Christa McDaniel, a petite brunette who, depending on her manner of dress, could have passed for an attorney or model. She worked as a realtor with Century 21.

Keith had a crush on Christa, and when her warm hand met his, he blushed.

"Keith! How are you?"

"I'm fine, you?"

"You lying sonofabitch," Christa replied coyly.

"You can sense it, then?"

"Sense it? I can *see* it. You've got bags under your eyes the color of coal!"

Keith smiled wanly in reply. "Yeah. I guess I need this pretty bad. Worse than I'd like to admit."

Christa squeezed his hand. Keith thought of her blue eyes sparkling in the crisp night air.

"We *all* need this. I'm glad you're here. I guess we both know what it's like to be married to nonbelievers."

The wind began to increase, rippling the small portion of the lake that remained unfrozen. The light rain suddenly abated.

"It's beginning," Christa said, smiling beautifully up at Keith. He gripped her hand tightly.

Three sea-blue pinpoints of light appeared over the lake and began to spin in unison around an invisible axis. The line fell silent. The speed of the lights began to increase, growing into an audible hum. At the peak of the frequency an iridescent corridor of light cracked the ice covering the lake and drilled down into the dark water below.

The light began to pulsate from red to blue to green, and Keith felt Christa clench his hand intensely. His pulse quickened. Across the line, the old gang from Hallowell High smiled like drunk children.

Suddenly, the Angel of the Lake ascended in its timeless grace from the corridor, the bony membrane of its wings and bare ribcage reflecting the prismatic display. It was the color of algae-slicked marble. Two sea-blue pinpoints of light drifted languidly in the eye sockets. A blue glow emanated from within the skeletal chest.

For a moment it hovered before them in its otherworldly radiance, spinning softly as thin beams of blue light made a connection with the twenty-eight pairs of eyes on the water's edge. Keith thought briefly about the days before the dark angel's arrival, days when the group members were not only judge and jury of the soul being sacrificed to joy, but also the executioners. Keith wasn't sure what had brought the entity to their sacred lake; perhaps, he thought, it was the combined desire of twenty-seven souls screaming across the dimensional abyss for a representative to perform a job that required an inhuman degree of coldness. *In any case, it's better this way,* thought Keith, *cleaner this way.* Then the precise light pierced Keith's pupils, and he no longer had thoughts of his own, but the thoughts of everyone.

With a sound like the creaking of old timbers, the dark angel ascended into the night sky over Lake Hallowell, and the eyes and thoughts of the Hallowell gang flew with it.

—

Sylvia sat up suddenly in bed. Mitch, her husband, snored beside her.

"Merry Christmas, you fat bastard," she said, scornfully, as she rose out of bed. She grabbed a pack of Lady Slims from the dresser and walked over to the wet bar, the only wedding gift that seemed to matter anymore, to mix a drink.

Sylvia noticed a distant ringing sound. At first, she attributed it to the clinking of the ice cubes as she stirred her vodka tonic, but when she paused to listen, the sound continued. She was reminded of her childhood and staying up late on Christmas Eve to await the sound of jingle bells on Santa's sleigh.

For a moment Sylvia considered waking Mitch; he kept a silver-plated .357 in his nightstand. Yet the beauty of the sound mesmerized her, and she reconsidered. Her heart began to race in anticipation.

Sylvia reached the top of the staircase. A moment later, the tumbler of vodka fell silently onto the thick shag carpet as she gasped.

A skeletal angel hovered in the living room, haloed by blue light. It was horrific in its beauty.

The entity awaited the silent affirmation of the Hallowell gang, the silent approval that said *Yes, hers is the soul almost extinguished by sin . . . this is the soul you will take to round out our own.* Acting as a spiritual conduit, the entity transmitted the thoughts, feelings, and memories of Sylvia's mottled, gray spirit to the twenty-eight presences that ringed the lake.

For a moment, time was suspended.

There was a still woman by a stair railing and a still horror floating in her living room and twenty-seven still spirits by the still waters of a silent lake.

Then the varied voices of Hallowell High spoke up in unison. A simple command: *Yes.*

Needle-thin twin beams of light illuminated from the being's sapphire eyes to meet Sylvia's own. She felt herself drawn forward.

A sudden flash of blinding white light glowed behind her eyes. Sylvia placed her hands on her temple and winced. The images came then, a swirling mosaic of life. The young families from the community were all familiar. There were birthday parties, pizza nights, soccer teams, and Disneyland vacations.

The angel raised her and Sylvia felt the tip of one toe brush against the oak banister as she was carried forward and upward.

More images followed. She witnessed graduations, lovemaking, anniversaries, trick-or-treaters, and games of hide-and-seek awash in an avalanche of joy and laughter.

In an instant the images dissolved into a vacuum, a woman floating in front of a mirror—face wrinkled and hair frosted with age. The sense of her loneliness was utterly profound. It hurt her head and broke her heart.

The angel averted its gaze, and before Sylvia broke her neck on the tiles below, she smiled sincerely for the first time in years.

—

Shocked gasps erupted from the group upon witnessing the impact of the Sylvia's fall. For a moment, a heaviness the scent of sadness filled the air. Another moment passed before the group members realized that they had returned to their bodies.

Pandemonium followed—embraces, shouts, and kisses swept across the believers like a wave. Keith held Christa for a long time as tears streamed down his face.

The Angel of the Lake was returned to its resting place beneath the dark water.

Through Sylvia's cleanse of their lives, they had been given back their precious memories; joy had returned to the group, and they all felt profound gratitude as they mentally stretched out before themselves the hours that they would carry for a year, before their own degradation emptied them once again.

They, all of them, shared the same hope: *Maybe I'll do better this year, and next year I won't need this.*

But they knew they wouldn't.

The Night Fighter

IT WAS a foggy night at Dover Airfield.

Tendrils of mist hovered around the sleek fuselage of the Supermarine Spitfire like the ghost of spent exhaust. At the far end of the airfield, two mechanics worked on the radial engines of a Boeing B-17. Their low voices and the metallic rattle of tools were muffled and swallowed up by the dead air. High above, the dull stars formed endless runways to the gods.

No one noticed the lean stranger as he stalked across the field. Unlike the others who lived and worked there, he bore no uniform, insignia or medals, and his walk was fluid like an animal's, not a controlled military step.

The stranger had tread upon this field long before men had christened the isle Britain; he had walked the circles at Stonehenge before the Druids gave it blood.

Despite it all, the stranger had never been inside one of the metal predators which shrieked across the English Channel to meet the German bombers before they dropped their deadly cargo over London.

The stranger had watched the planes take flight many times from the edge of the woods and had stolen a flight manual from the barracks. He had read, misunderstood, and read again.

Finally, he was ready to fly.

He loped up to the lone fighter and pressed his hands against the cool metal skin. He had experienced an eon of sensations over many centuries—arctic winds and Caribbean breezes, smooth marble and grainy sandstone being but a few—but nothing had ever felt as new or as alien as this sleek machine.

His long, pale, curved fingers grabbed the flaps and he pulled himself upward onto the wing. His taut and sinuous frame slid into the cockpit, and he pulled the canopy shut.

A sea of gages, dials, buttons, and levers confronted him. Slowly, the images and words returned.

Altimeter.

Artificial horizon.

Airspeed.

Pitch.

He switched on the ignition. The engine coughed and sputtered like an old, asthmatic man, shattering the dew-laden stillness. Finally, the engine evened out and achieved its characteristic purr.

From the far end of the field, the two mechanics ran toward him, their flashlights, low stars on the darkened field. *What was wrong?* The stranger asked himself, looking about the tight cockpit desperately. *Why won't it fly?*

The mechanics closed in on the fighter. The stranger's keen ears heard the thud of their boots on the pavement growing louder with every step.

He cleared his mind and concentrated. The pages concerning take-off procedures filtered back into his mind's eye.

He groped wildly among the controls for the wheel brakes as the mechanics' flashlights shone through the narrow windscreens and onto his face. The work lights felt to him like miniature suns going supernova on his cheeks.

The stranger howled in agony and yanked on the wheel brake release, ripping it from the instrument panel in his fury.

"Jesus!" one of the mechanics cried, seeing the wild shock of coal black hair and the contorted ivory face.

The plane climbed over the wheel blocks and dragged itself forward.

One of the mechanics was hit in the stomach by the wing. He grunted and fell over. The second tripped in panic and fell into the whirling blades of the outer right motor's propeller.

The pale pilot watched in fascination, easing the throttle forward and running a slender pink tongue over his lips as crimson streams of blood sprayed across the canopy.

He controlled his thirst and turned away as the plane's speed increased.

Sixty miles per hour.

Seventy.

The stranger panicked as the nose of the aircraft lowered toward the earth. He soon realized it was merely the natural motion of the tail leaving the runway.

Eighty.

Ninety.

One hundred.

He eased the flight stick back at 110 miles per hour and the Supermarine Spitfire took flight. In a fit of exhilaration, the stranger threw open the canopy and let the wind streamline his hair and fill his pores.

The matchbox fields of England grew small beneath him as he headed for the dark band of the distant Channel.

He swooped, banked, dove, and pitched the protesting plane toward the horizon. Recalling the trigger, he sent machine gun bursts burning through the sky. He observed the sleek radar towers which lined England's coast and admired them in the way he'd sometimes marvel at castles along the Rhine.

And somewhere near the French side of the Channel, he found the moon.

It hung suspended above the clouds like the pearl earring of the sky. The moon, that ancient timepiece which pulled him from graves and the cathedral catacombs at dusk for another night of bloodlust. Tears from narrow eyes spilled like red wine and were sucked into the 350 miles per hour wind as he contemplated his even paler sister.

There was a burning in his soul not unlike mortal desire as he pushed the flight stick forward and the plane into a dive. The aircraft groaned under the stress, and he squinted his eyes as the air surrounding him shrieked and the turbulent waters of the Channel filled his vision.

A string of rivets popped loose where the wing met the fuselage. Still he dove.

Finally, he pulled back hard on the flight stick and began the steep ascent toward Luna.

This was how he wanted to end the centuries of blood feasts, like an inverted Prometheus, heading for union with his heavenly soulmate.

The moon grew very large in the windshield, her pleasing, cratered form beautiful and delicate. Maybe, he considered, if he willed with a millennium of wishes he might reach eternal night.

The engines suddenly coughed and the plane sputtered to a stall. The propellers spun listlessly, and the craft started falling once again toward far-distant whitecaps.

He pulled everything, clicked everything, but it was no use. He lowered the landing gear and the flaps. He fired shells into the sky and heard the electric hiss of the radio.

Nothing could stop his descent to the sea.

The wind sucked at him demonically, and his face was pulled

backward by gravitational force, revealing two long, curved, slick fangs in lieu of eyeteeth.

The plane's structure began to fail. The loose wing sheared off the fuselage with a banshee's wail and disappeared into the darkness.

At the last moment he sprung from the plane. There was a sound like water rushing back to its source and a *pop!* as the plane fell away.

A moment of stillness ensued before the plane exploded against the water.

A small black shape began winging its way over the Channel toward occupied France, its mouse-like head refusing to turn and look at the moon which hovered placidly above.

It flew through the night. The exercise left it quite famished, quite thirsty.

Pumpkin Seed Spit

BRIAN AND Ria waited near the stop sign at the intersection of Wofford Lane and Marlboro Way. Brian wore black and white face paint and a skeleton shirt. Ria was adorned in a pointy witch hat and cape. The pillowcases in their hands for collecting candy were empty.

"Where is he?" Brian asked, impatiently.

"He'll be out soon; chill out. You know what his dad's like," Ria replied.

A door slammed and Matt bolted from his house. Sniffling, he wiped tears from his eyes. Matt wore green sweats and green dishwashing gloves. He carried a latex alien mask in his hands.

"You okay, Matt?" Ria asked.

Matt put on a good face. "Yeah, just another fight between my parents," he said stoically, taking Ria's hand when she offered it to him. She always made him feel better.

"Alright then," said Brian, the unspoken leader of the group, "let's get this horror show on the road."

"Sorry for the delay, guys," Matt said, apologetically. "I betcha the good candy is already gone."

Brian slapped Matt's shoulder. "You're in luck, buddy. This year it's not about candy. This year we have a shot at eating lunch with the eighth graders."

"What are you talking about?" Matt asked.

Ria interjected. "The eighth graders made some stupid dare with Brian that if we see The Pumpkin Tree they'll let us eat lunch at their table."

"You guys can't be serious!" Matt asked. "That thing is a myth. I say we go trick-or-treating like every year."

Ria squeezed Matt's hand and offered a supportive smile.

"Why, exactly, would we want to eat lunch with those guys?" Matt asked. "Most of 'em are jerks."

"They're always treating us like little kids. This time they'll be forced to take us seriously," Brian asserted. "Anyway, you two can act like grade schoolers if you want. I'm going for The Pumpkin Tree." Brian took off down Marlboro Way. Ria shrugged before she and Matt reluctantly followed along.

The trio received curious looks as it marched determinedly past parents and other trick-or-treaters, never once stopping at any of the houses to amass confections. Brian's pace was relentless. Matt and Ria struggled to keep up.

"Slow down, Brian!" Ria said.

"What's the rush?" Matt asked.

Brian swung around and glared at them. "Do you guys actually want to walk through the woods in the dark? Not me. We probably have thirty minutes until sunset."

"How would we even prove we found The Pumpkin Tree?" asked Ria.

Without answering, Brian held up his cellphone, pointing at it for emphasis, and marched on.

They walked and walked. Matt and Ria looked longingly at the yards and porches decorated with garish orange lights, blow molds, plastic tombstones, and inflatable ghouls.

The October afternoon was unusually warm, and they were all sweating as Marlboro Way became an uphill climb. Finally, they reached the dead end of the road and began following a small dirt trail into the woods. Soon the narrow path widened to a gravel road where a great clearing stretched out in both directions. Every several hundred yards they passed the hum of a transmission tower. The massive pylons extended to the darkening sky as if pleading to the heavens.

After the clearing, the small dirt path resumed. Eventually, the three friends emerged from the woods and reached the high school's parking lot.

"Let's rest here," Brian said.

They all sat down on the curb. Ria shared a package of M&M's she had brought from home.

For several moments, the gang was content to rest and munch.

Matt finally spoke. "Brian, what if this is all a joke? What if the eighth graders are playing us? We'll be the laughing stocks of the school, and we'll totally miss out on Halloween."

"Don't you think I've thought about that?" Brian fired back. "Man, you guys must think I'm an idiot. I'm hoping it *is* a joke. Here's the plan: We go in, take a photo of some creepy-looking tree, and tell them we found The Pumpkin Tree. The joke will be on them when they try to find it!"

"I don't know, Brian," Ria said. "I think they're smarter than that."

"Remember, I'm a year older and wiser than both of you," Brian countered.

"Only because you were held back a grade," Matt replied.

Brian raised a fist as if to punch Matt. The younger boy shrunk back against the curb.

"Alright, let's get moving. The woods get really thick beyond the sewer pipe." Brian stood up and brushed dirt from his jeans.

"The sewer pipe?" Ria gulped.

"Relax," Brian said, "I've gone through it a hundred times. It's wide enough that we can walk through without hunching down."

Brain hurried across the parking lot. Ria and Matt halfheartedly followed. Soon they entered the woods on the opposite side of the lot.

It was getting later and darker. There was no path. The branches and brambles scratched and stung. Matt looked back at Ria and shook his head as they continued on.

The sewer pipe was nearly six feet in circumference. Brian switched on the LED flash of his iPhone, though it did little to cut through the enveloping darkness. They tried to straddle the concrete pipe as much as possible to avoid the stream of murky water running down the middle, but inevitably ended up with soaked shoes and socks.

Finally, they reached the other side. But twilight was upon them and the dusky sky only provided meager light in the deep woods.

Brian scrambled up one of the muddy banks of the stream that was fed by the pipe. He squinted into the darkness ahead.

"I think I see something," Brian exclaimed.

"Sure you do," Ria replied. She felt dirty and exhausted as she scaled the slippery bank.

"Good one, Brian," echoed Matt. "You really got us that time."

"No, I'm serious! C'mere!" he insisted.

They joined Brian on the bank and followed his outstretched hand. At first the light was so subtle as to be insignificant, but after staring at it for several moments, none could deny the orange flickering glow in the distance.

"Okay," said Ria, "I've seen enough horror movies to know that a campfire in the middle of the woods on Halloween night is never a good thing. We should get out of here now," she urged.

"You two can sissy out if you want," Brian said. "I didn't walk all this way for nothing." He stormed ahead, oblivious to the noise he made while tramping through the undergrowth.

"He's the definition of a bull in a china closet!" Matt exclaimed. "So much for the element of surprise."

Ria gripped Matt's hand again. "C'mon, let's go see this tree."

"Guys, c'mon! You won't believe this," Brian exclaimed in the distance.

Bumbling through the last thicket of branches, they joined him in a small clearing.

An ancient, colossal tree stood before them, limbs extended in all directions. Its bark consisted of thick, dark fissures and deep striations. It bore no leaves, but dozens of jack-o-lanterns, lit by flickering candles, hung from countless branches.

For several long minutes the kids stood in silent awe.

"I don't believe it. The Pumpkin Tree is … is real," Brian said.

"Who did this?" Matt asked in disbelief.

"Eighth graders," whispered Ria.

"No. They could never pull this off," said Brian. "Probably the work of some local college."

"I don't know. Seems like an awful lot of work," Matt replied.

Suddenly, the limbs of the tree creaked, the tree twisted, and its crown bent over them. The jack-o-lanterns rocked violently from side to side.

Matt, Ria, and Matt stared in astonished fear.

"Good lord," Brian whispered.

"Silence!" a guttural voice cried from a dark, jagged opening in the tree's trunk. "You are in the presence of The Pumpkin Tree. For countless generations have I existed. For countless generations shall I remain."

The kids instinctively stepped back, but were met by a network of thorny branches that felt as strong as steel cables against their spines.

"There is no escaping The Pumpkin Tree," the plant spoke, its foul breath reeking of decay and death.

"Wh-what do you want?" Brian asked.

"You will return to your night's activities and, in so doing, distribute my seeds. Approach!" the tree demanded.

Against their will, and propelled by the branches that ensnared them, the children advanced to the awful maw of the tree.

Brian and Matt held out their open pillowcases. Ria stood in a daze.

"Ria!" Matt insisted. "Ria! We have to do what it says!"

Finally, Ria held her out her pillowcase, turning her face away from The Pumpkin Tree in disgust.

The Pumpkin Tree inhaled with such force that Ria had to grab her pointed hat to avoid it being sucked into its gaping jaws. An awful exhalation followed as the tree rapidly spat a several dozen pumpkin seeds into each pillowcase. Despite remaining mostly empty, the slipcovers were so weighty that the kids had to struggle, white knuckled, to avoid dropping them to the ground.

The tree then breathed over them with a sickly, intoxicating breath that stunk of rotted gourds, fermented earth, and terror.

"Go!" it demanded, loosening the network of branches that held them prisoner.

Brian, Ria, and Matt quickly retraced their steps as they made the long journey home, remembering little of the details. The sewer pipe, the electrical pylons, the path through the woods—it all seemed effortless as the moon traced their trek from high above. It was well past seven o'clock, and they were in full darkness, but even that seemed more of a comfort than a hindrance.

Upon reaching the first house near a dead end, they knocked and said in unison, "Trick-or-Treat!" As fifty-year-old Henry Armitage opened the front door, Brian unearthed his bag. The middle-aged man frowned at the kids before starting to mutter something about the lateness of the hour. Armitage gazed into Brian's bag of seeds and was immediately mesmerized. An orange energy tendril spiraled upward, carrying a single seed into Armitage's mouth.

Brian, Matt, and Ria wanted to scream, but found it impossible. While their souls were wrenched into knots by the horror they witnessed, outwardly they stood emotionless, even tranquil, as layers of skin and flesh melted away until all that remained of Henry Armitage was a living skeleton.

When the transformation was complete, they advanced to the next house. Ria shared the seeds, and Asenath Waite, a young mother of two, was hideously transformed into a witch with boils, green teeth, and trail of lesions across her forehead.

Matt was next to present The Pumpkin Tree's offering to the world. Three seeds were received by a couple and their young baby. Within moments they became a trio of giant pale, eyeless larvae that oozed and squiggled out of their clothes.

The kids continued their dark pilgrimage late into the night, all along Marlboro Way, up Wofford Lane, and across the great loop of Limestone Place. They then visited the homes out on Metzerott Road that stretched to the edge of the interstate.

They continued until they were left with three empty pillowcases.

Just before midnight, they were dragged, spellbound, back through the woods and the creek to The Pumpkin Tree.

As before, the tree greeted them with its awful, thorny embrace.

"Excellent, children. Excellent!" the tree croaked, clasping two short branches together like hands. "Tonight begins a new age of monsters, the likes of which Earth has not beheld since my last sojourn, centuries ago. You believe your bags to be empty, but I am not so unkind. Look again," the tree urged.

Still entranced, Matt, Ria, and Brian each gazed inside their pillowcases. Orange tendrils of light like vines reached up and forced open their throats, bringing with the light a single seed for each to consume.

The Pumpkin Tree shook and laughed deeply as the children changed. Its limbs clicked together like the cracking of teeth.

Moments later, the tree bent over a skeleton, witch, and swamp creature approvingly.

"Flee this place. You are now monsters in the purest sense and must, until the end of your days, dwell in shadow, in darkness. Never forget that you are, and shall forever be, in my debt. Remember me, my brethren, especially on the Eve of All Hallows."

The creatures that had been Matt, Ria, and Brian slowly nodded, understanding and embracing their fate.

"Flee!" the tree roared.

Without a moment's hesitation, the three creatures escaped into the darkness.

A Night for Animals

LATE AFTERNOON sunlight filtered down through the treetops, gilding the woods with gold. Sounds of children playing, and gentle conversation, drifted across the campground, as did an argument.

"Go ahead and leave then. I sure as hell can't put up with your crap anymore!"

With this, Craig stood straight up and took a deep chug of beer, ignoring the weeping woman before him.

Kaitlyn waited for him to recant the words, waited for an apology acknowledging that he'd gone too far, said too much.

It never came. Craig's verbal assault hung in the air, suspended in her mind, a scar like the hundreds of other disappointments that characterized her failing marriage. *What had happened? Where was the kind, caring man she had fallen in love with? The gentle, thoughtful spouse?*

Gone. Kaitlyn bit her lip, using her pride to hold back the steady flow of tears, and started up the trail away from the campsite.

—

Twilight had arrived by the time Kaitlyn finally took a break from walking. The homey, familiar sounds of the campground were miles distant. She was now surrounded by the solitude of the woods.

Sitting down atop a fallen tree in the path, Kaitlyn began to rub her arms for warmth. She wished she had brought along a sweatshirt, but it had taken her full reserve to simply leave him behind.

Kaitlyn took a deep breath and looked around. She was alone for the first time in longer than she could remember. No kids, no boss, no bridge club, *no husband*—just herself.

The path continued to climb sharply up the mountain, narrowing some twenty yards above her current position.

For a moment, she considered heading back. But then she realized that Craig would be there, feeling no remorse and, in all likelihood, polishing off the rest of the twelve pack. He might even strike her. Kaitlyn knew it was in her best interest to keep moving ahead.

The going was more difficult now, and she often had to push away branches and briars to continue up the mountain.

Suddenly, goosebumps rose on Kaitlyn's skin, and she sensed someone close by, watching her. Kaitlyn turned quickly to see a dark shape running away into the trees. She froze.

A squirrel darted into view on a nearby tree trunk, and then scampered up into the tangle of branches overhead.

She wasn't sure if she'd seen a dark shape or if it had the imagined result of exhaustion, anger, and grief.

You're going batty, Sister. Completely Looney Tunes.

Kaitlyn giggled, rubbed her eyes, and walked on.

—

She had been walking for miles. The elevation had increased during the hike, and occasional breaks in the trees offered glimpses of the valley below.

Twilight arrived, and under the rich growth of trees it was almost night. The weedy undergrowth along the path seemed to grab at Kaitlyn's boots and ankles with every step.

An owl hooted in the distance, and Kaitlyn stopped to listen to the woods move around her. She wondered what types of creatures roamed the forest at night.

Whatever they are, she thought, *they can't be worse than the one inhabiting my campsite. I'll live up here off the land before I return to him.*

Despite her resolute determination, apprehension remained. The mountaintop was no place to spend an October night. Her legs were stiff and numb from the exertion of the hike, but they were failing. Shelter or not, she would have to soon stop for the night.

At that moment, Kaitlyn observed a light in the distance.

—

Kaitlyn stood at the clearing and savored her first look at the cabin. Lavish stained-glass windows contrasted strongly with the dark timber that ran along its side. A thread of smoke drifted into the night sky from a stone chimney.

Kaitlyn shivered in the cold mountain air. The cabin was lovely, but it belonged to someone. What could she tell the occupants? Certainly not the truth. They'd be likely to question her sanity, hiking halfway up a mountain over an argument.

The wind picked up and Kaitlyn's stomach rumbled. She hadn't eaten in hours.

Hating herself for what she was about to do, Kaitlyn began to approach the cabin.

Without fully knowing why, Kaitlyn suddenly stopped. The goosebumps were back, and the hairs along her cervical spine stood up on end. Her stomach felt like a ball of ice.

And then she heard it—a low growl that arose from behind her.

Kaitlyn turned, and the beast was upon her. She clutched its black mass of fur and could smell the fresh kill of an animal as its breath plumed out from a snarling mouth, could see the rage in its crimson eyes.

Overpowered, both in weight and strength, Kaitlyn quickly fell.

—

A burning sensation on her lips roused Kaitlyn from an unconscious slumber.

"Ouch!" she cried out.

"Please forgive me. Your lips are chapped from the wind. I thought, perhaps, warm tea would do you some good."

Kaitlyn opened her eyes and was glad she did.

Before her stood the finest-looking man she had ever seen. The stranger was tall and slim, with a slight beard and mocha brown hair. His skin was slightly olive, with reddish-brown undertones.

"Are you okay?" he asked, gazing down at Kaitlyn.

His blue-grey eyes seemed to shift color as he stared at Kaitlyn.

"Yes—yes, thank you. Where am I? What's happened?"

"I'm afraid Louis frightened you. He is an excellent hound, but somewhat overprotective of the cabin. I'm very sorry. We don't often get visitors up here."

Kaitlyn sat up, only then aware that she was resting atop a bed. "Where is ... Louis?"

"I let him out for the night. I was afraid he'd upset you."

"That may be the understatement of the year," Kaitlyn said, smiling. "Your cabin is gorgeous." Her eyes drank in fine artwork hanging from the walls and silver fruit bowls atop an oak table.

"Thank you. It's all I have, besides Louis, of course. I do try to keep it up. Would you care for tea?"

Kaitlyn looked down into the brimming cup and inhaled the scent of raspberries.

"Yes, thank you very much. Excuse my manners, it's been quite a night. My name is Kaitlyn."

"Anthony Dubois," he replied, extending a dark, supple hand.

Kaitlyn clasped it with her own. A warmth seemed to roar through her blood as she held his hand. Her heart began to race and she felt slightly faint.

"Dubois? Is that French?" Kaitlyn asked.

"Yes, my mother was French. My father was from Nepal."

Kaitlyn nodded. "I'm very sorry to have disturbed you, Mr. Dubois. I simply lost my way in the woods while hiking. It would be impossibly rude of me to stay."

"Nonsense. At least get your strength back. Drink the tea; it will warm you."

Kaitlyn lifted the china to her lips and drank deeply.

It tasted of chocolate, sassafras, and raspberry. It seemed to permeate every part of her body with warmth. The light-headed sensation returned, but this time it was a pleasurable feeling.

The cabin was dimly lit. It occurred to Kaitlyn that Anthony's beard seemed to thicken before her eyes. There was something else, too. While he had previously stood over the bed, he now seemed to be hunched over it. She was almost certain of this because his face was much closer to hers now.

Kaitlyn struggled to keep her eyes open. She felt so good on the bed, so wonderfully safe and comfortable. *Perhaps,* she thought, *I'm already dreaming.*

Moments passed. Kaitlyn watched as Anthony continued to transform in front of her. Tufts of hair grew out of his ears, his lower jaw stretched forward out of his face, and his eyes pulsed red.

Kaitlyn felt that whether she was awake, asleep, or in the hypnagogic state somewhere in the waking and dreaming worlds, that she should do … something. But she couldn't move. So wonderfully, wonderfully comfortable was Kaitlyn at this moment.

Anthony tilted his head back and howled. It was a gentle, reverberating echo in Kaitlyn's head, like blue waves lapping against the shore. He seemed to be grinning as he opened his mouth, revealing spiky rows of ivory teeth. He leaned closer and bit into Kaitlyn's neck.

Kaitlyn moaned softly as the blood flowed out of her, not caring if Anthony heard her or not. The sensation felt like her first child toying gently with her teat during feedings. It was an exquisite dream, so wonderfully, wonderfully comfortable…

—

Two dark forms slithered quietly around the campsite, their padded feet hushed in the dry bed of leaves.

Craig, seated with his head down atop the picnic table, heard the distant sound and turned slightly. In his current state, movement wasn't easy.

"Christ, Kaitlyn, I'm sslorrry," he slurred. "Slelp me to bed."

A breeze stole through the clearing, causing the tent flap to beat gently against the nylon tent.

"Kaitlyn?" Craig asked again, slowly lifting his head off of the table.

Two shapes crept by the tent.

"Kaitlyn?"

The shapes paused in the woods—a large, male black wolf and a smaller gray female. The female cocked her head in misunderstanding. The harvest moon above provided an eerie backdrop to the silent play. The male showed his teeth and held a paw out toward the picnic table in the clearing. The female nodded.

The grey wolf began to creep up behind Craig.

There was a clatter as the wind picked up and blew several empty cans off of the picnic table.

Craig stood up and turned.

"Kaitlyn?" he asked.

"Yessss," the she-wolf replied. She leapt, fur silvered by the moonlight, and tore into Craig's throat with inhuman barbarity.

—

Two shapes walked through the darkened woods.

"Do you feel better?" Anthony asked.

"Yes," Kaitlyn replied, uncomfortably walking upright on her new feet, still not quite recognizing the sound of her own voice. "I don't feel lost anymore."

Anthony nodded, supporting Kaitlyn as she awkwardly made her way. There was a break in the tree line, and the moon hung fat and heavy in the sky. Anthony gazed upward and tilted his head back in an ear-piercing howl. Kaitlyn joined him, as did the dogs in the campsites down

in the valley below and the wolf packs above them.
It was a night for animals, and they were content.

The Man Next Door

WHEN I think back to what happened, I sometimes still can't believe it wasn't a dream. But every so often I walk by the remains of the house, his house, and the smell of coriander around the foundation takes me back to 1977 and I know that it happened. It was real.

—

Dad pulled the bright yellow Ryder truck through the quiet suburban streets of Sun Terrace. It was an early Sunday morning, August 1977. In the distance a lawn mower droned its way through the morning. I suspect it woke more than a few residents.

We finally reached 9202 Thacker Way. It had been a long, tiresome drive, but I was wired on soda and chocolate bars. I bounded out of the passenger side as soon as my mom opened the door. She and dad unfolded themselves slowly and stretched as the morning sun shone overhead.

Mom walked to the front door of our new home as dad raised the truck's roll-up door and unfurled the loading ramp. Unloading the Ryder was hard work, especially for me, but our moods were light despite the strain on our bodies and the sweat that soon followed.

I wonder if that was the first time he saw us. I can imagine him staring out the window from the second story, deep-set green eyes gazing at our every step.

An hour into unpacking I stumbled into the kitchen and dropped a box on the floor.

"I'm bushed," I said, and dropped onto the carpet.

"C'mon, Billy. There are only a few more," dad said with a wink.

"Geez. I never knew we owned so much stuff."

"Let's get the last few boxes outta the Ryder and then break for

Big Macs and fries."

"Great!" I said, excited by the thought of eating junk food.

We headed back outside and saw mom bending down to pick up broken pieces of china that littered the driveway.

"Relax, honey," dad said. "It's nothing a little Krazy Glue won't fix."

"Charles Thomas! This set came from my mother."

"All the more reason not to worry about it," dad chuckled as I stifled a laugh of my own.

"Honestly, Charles, that isn't a nice thing to say, especially in front of Billy."

"Okay, I apologize. It was just a joke. Let's finish up so we can eat."

We moved around to the back of the truck where five or six boxes rested atop the driveway.

Dad bent down, picked up a box labeled BILLY'S ATARI in purple magic marker, and handed it to me.

"Think you can handle this?"

"Heck yeah!" I said enthusiastically. At the time, the Atari game console was the king of all toys.

Once inside the house I placed the box on the living room floor. My scrawny, twelve-year-old arms were aching, and I didn't want to move any more boxes, so I snuck out to the backyard. A moment later I bent down and spied a caterpillar winding its way up a lean blade of grass.

A moment later I felt a prickle on my back. At first I thought I'd been stung, but the sensation was all wrong. It felt as if I'd had been struck by an ice cube. Instinctively, I whipped my head around.

Over the hedge that separated our lawn and the house next door, a face peered down at me from a second-story window. The face seemed incredibly to me, even older than my grandfather's face had looked just before he died. There was something about the eyes. Even through the glass they shone green. It gave me the creeps.

A second later, a long, contorted arm reached drew down the shade.

I wasted no time running to my parents.

"Mom! Dad! Did you see it?" I yelled.

"See what?" Mom asked.

"The old man next door," I stammered. "He was staring at me. It was *creepy!*"

"Listen, Billy," Mom replied, "whomever he is, that man is our neighbor. I don't think he'd appreciate being called old, even if it's true."

"But—"

"Your mom's right, Billy," Dad said sternly.

"Yeah, but—"

"No buts. Understood?"

"Yeah," I said, glumly.

"Good. Let's lock up and head out. The rest of the stuff can wait."

We piled into the Dodge Caravan that Dad had driven down to the house the day before. Soon our talk turned to fries, hamburgers, and milkshakes, but I couldn't shake the feeling that the old man was trouble.

As we approached our driveway on the ride home, I turned around to look at the old man's house, fully expecting him to be watching our approach. But only the house stared back at him, shuttered tightly from the outside.

—

The next day was Monday and my first day at the new school. I had no time to think about the old man with the cool green eyes, though I purposely walked on the other side of the street on my way to the bus stop to keep as far away from his house as possible.

I made new friends with ease, and by Wednesday had assembled a small group of pals at school, including Steve Atkins, whom I considered to be my new best friend. Life was also going well for Mom and Dad. Dad had been assigned a big case at his new law firm. He even managed to find a tennis partner. Mom enjoyed her new teaching job at the local community college and was thrilled by her students' willingness to learn and their generally warm attitude. Overall, the first week in our new house was the perfect picture of suburban bliss.

Then I had the dream.

It was a Sunday night, and the breeze had picked up outside so that it covered the noise of the crickets. I'd been tossing and turning restlessly, unable to sleep because my parents had allowed me to stay up with them and watch *Duel*. I found myself thinking about the crazed, mysterious driver and his menacing Peterbilt truck. Finally I drifted off into slumber.

I think that part of the reason the dream was so terrible was that at first I didn't know if I was awake or asleep.

In the dream, I walked over to the window that looked out over the hedge and the house next door. The moon was full moon, and in the tall, distant trees that delineated the woods at the bottom of the street, huge, bird-like creatures sat hunched over the branches. Although there was no breeze, from somewhere down below I heard the sound of rustling leaves.

I looked down and saw with horror that the hedge was growing, towering upward into the night in a tangle of vines and branches that drew ever closer to me. Beneath the hedge I saw a silhouetted form growing and stretching along with the vines.

I then noticed a pair of eyes, cool and green, pulsing like emeralds as they rose swiftly with the branches toward me. The eyes belonged to the old man, and the old man was one with the hedge, his legs enmeshed with the bottom of the hedge, his fingers extending forth into sinuous appendages.

Silently the windows shattered. I screamed, but my scream carried no sound. I was ensnared within a cold, oaken grip that lifted me high into the night. The bird-creatures were now spiraling above and toward me, talons outstretched, and I was theirs to devour.

I woke in a cold sweat and glanced around my room. All was still. Hesitantly, I stepped out of bed and approached the window. All was well. I returned to my bed and pulled up the blankets, but sleep did not return for a long time.

—

I mentioned the old man at breakfast the next morning.

"Did you guys ever notice that our neighbor never comes out of his house?" I said tentatively, mouth half full of Frosted Flakes.

"Billy—" Dad began.

"I think he's evil. Maybe a vampire or something. Maybe that's why he always keeps his shades down."

"I think someone has an overactive imagination. He's … eccentric. That's all." Dad returned his attention to the morning newspaper.

"What does eccentric mean?" I asked.

"It's another word for weird or … unusual," Mom said

Dad raised an eyebrow and reentered the conversation. "All I'm saying is, whatever he does is his own business, as long as he's not breaking the law."

"Is blood sucking against the law?"

Dad shook his head in frustration as Mom tried hard not to crack up.

"Gotta go. See you all tonight," Dad said. He rose from the table, gave Mom a kiss, grabbed his suit jacket, and was out the door.

"Try not to let the neighbor bother you," Mom said.

I nodded and finished eating before heading out to the bus stop. Regardless of my parents' assurances, I intended to keep my distance from the house next door.

—

That night we were invited to dinner by the Middletons, a retired couple who lived on our block.

I wasn't looking forward it. What kid wants to spend the evening listening to a group of adults talk about adult things? I also had to take a bath and wear dress clothes. Doing homework would have been better.

It turned out I was pleasantly surprised by the Middletons, particularly Mr. Middleton, who I learned had flown a B-17 fighter plane in World War II.

As the plates were being cleared for dessert, I blurted out: "Mr. Middleton, do you know anything about the old man who lives next door to us?"

Mom and Dad looked aghast, and it was clear that Mr. Middleton could tell.

"It's okay. Billy's just a curious lad. Your neighbor—Judd Brown—is the sort of man who raises eyebrows. He keeps himself locked up in his house as if he were dead. Makes one wonder how he passes his days."

"I think he's a vampire," I quipped.

"That certainly would explain a few things," chuckled Mr. Middleton. "Mr. Brown used to be a friendly fellow. He was a night watchman at the Jones Museum in downtown, so he slept during the daylight hours. He and his wife divorced a long time ago, but he had a daughter who came by once or twice to see him. Last I recall, she passed away." Mr. Middleton shook his head slowly.

"Even back then—that was around 1955—he seemed old. Real old. I can't imagine him now. Must be in a wretched state, poor fellow. I suspect he's over 100 years of age by now, maybe older."

"Have you ever seen him go out for groceries, household goods?" Dad asked.

"Not recently. I suppose he has his food delivered. He uses a lawn service, so I know he's still alive and kicking."

"I saw him in the window," I announced.

"That so?" asked Mr. Middleton. "What did he look like?"

His eyes were . . . strange. The greenest eyes I'd ever seen."

"I'm sure old Judd was quite a sight." Mr. Middleton paused before continuing. "Have you noticed his hedge?"

"I've seen it," I said.

"He pays it a lot of attention. Lot of attention. You'll see. Lawn people stop by one or two times a month adding new topsoil. But I don't recall ever having seen it trimmed."

"Maybe its reached its maximum height," Mom suggested.

"No. It's a maple hedge. It's nowhere close to maximum height," Mr. Middleton said.

"It should be a big, tangled mess by now, unless Judd's going out there to cut it at midnight."

"Honestly, George!" Martha Middleton said.

"I call 'em like I see 'em," Mr. Middleton chuckled, breaking a serious, almost ghostly silence that had hung over the table as he spoke of Judd Brown.

We returned home an hour or so later. I expected Mom or Dad would lecture me on having brought up the old man, but they never did.

—

The following Monday morning, a pair of workmen arrived at Judd Brown's house in a battered pickup truck filled with sacks of peat moss and tanks of insecticide. I approached them on my way to the bus stop.

"Keep back, kid. Lotta dangerous pesticides here," the first worker, a lanky forty-something with a receding hairline warned. "Whacha want?"

"Do you know the man who lives here?"

"Judd Brown? Never met him." He lowered his voice and glanced cautiously in the direction of Brown's house. "Heard stories about him though. Strange stories."

"Like what?" I asked.

"Guy I work with named Charlie Storrie saw him once through the basement window on the far side of the house. Said Brown looked older than time itself and had more wrinkles than a thousand-year-old cypress."

"Geez," was all I could manage.

"Word of advice, kid: Stay the hell away from this place and the man who lives in it."

I turned away quickly and ran to the bus stop, never once looking back.

—

When I awoke the next morning it was still dark outside. The glowing hands of the Big Ben alarm clock on my night table read 2:15 At first I thought the wind had awakened me, but a moment later I heard the *feeling* behind the sound. There was no doubt it was coming from something alive. I laid in bed beneath blankets that did little to soothe my escalating fear.

After some time I cautiously rose from the bed and moved toward the window not sure what to expect. Overhead, the moon was a slim crescent while leaves hung listlessly on distant trees.

The sound returned, more audible now. A whimpering sigh rising in the night. I gazed left to the hedge separating our property from Judd Brown's. He was there in the back of his yard, as aged and frightening in appearance as I'd been led to believe. Gnarled and bent like a branch bearing too much weight. His eyes and were tomato green, and his long, weedy hair matched their hue. His body was a mix of burnt sienna and umber. He was stretched across the ground and pouring peat moss over his body repeatedly while moaning softly like a cat.

I was spellbound and unable to look away. As the Judd Brown's ritual continued, he began to change. His eyes pulsed and his cries grew wilder and predatory.

At that instant I knew I should have gotten Mom and Dad, but I couldn't turn away. I sensed that something was about to happen. Moments later, something did.

The old man's body, which had already looked tree-like, began to twist and contort as he morphed into something more vegetative than human. He unwound sinuous limbs from peat moss and rose slowly from the ground. With great effort, he lifted one stumpy leg and moved toward the hedge. He seemed to become one with the hedge, for soon I could not distinguish one from the other. Long minutes passed until, finally, he separated from the hedge and slowly returned to his house as long fingers, like serpentine branches, closed the front door.

I considered waking my parents, but what would I say? What proof could I offer? They'd dismiss my tale a mere nightmare and send me along back to bed. If I wanted to learn more about Judd Brown, I was going to have to do it on my own. With this realization, I crawled back under the blankets and replayed the scenes of the old man's actions over in my head many times before sleep finally reclaimed me.

—

Three weeks passed, during which time I made nightly attempts to sneak over to Mr. Brown's house only to give into my own fears each time and scurry home. Finally, I found the reserve to carry out a plan to not only see the old man up close but to snap a photo of him with my Polaroid One Step instant camera.

I crept across the yard and soon arrived at a first-floor window. The scent of coriander filled the air. Through a gap in the curtain, I could see into a dimly lit living room. Covered from floor to ceiling in greenery, it was unlike anything I'd ever seen. One wall was comprised of tall bamboo stalks while the others were a mixture of red twig dogwood and lilac.

Soon, Judd Brown lumbered into the room, accompanied by a slender, pale female with short, cropped hair. Unlike the old man, whose clothing was frayed and dirty, his companion's attire—a form-fitting black jumpsuit with purple suede high heels—was clean and unsullied. Although I couldn't hear the conversation that was taking place, the expressions on they wore made it apparent this was no celebration.

I quietly pushed my camera against the glass and peered through its lens and snapped a fast photo. In my haste, I'd forgotten about the camera's built-in flash. It erupted in a brilliant flare of light, drawing the attention of my subjects. I rose quickly and began to run, but suddenly I was no longer outside. In a heartbeat I found myself face to face with Judd Brown and his mysterious companion. It was only then, as I stood face to face with Brown, that I realized the extent of his inhumanity. I tried to run but my arms and legs were in stasis.

"Fan of yours?" the woman asked Brown.

"Neighbor kid," he said, voice audible gravel. "Lives next door."

"What's your name, neighbor kid?"

"Billy," I whispered.

"Billy." She sighed. "Mediocre. Was a time when a name mattered. Prometheus. Persephone. Athena. And this guy here. Isn't that right, Ampelos?"

Brown said nothing.

"Six-thousand years ago, give or take a hundred, young Ampelos here was tragically killed. I … resurrected him, transforming him into the Earth's first vine."

"I never asked you to—"

"Be silent. You've had an amazing run during your evolution, and you've managed to elude me all these centuries. It's time to return to the flock, Ampelos. Time to be rejoin your beloved Dionysus."

"Dionysus?" Brown said, his limbs slowly retracted, and his green eyes dimmed.

"I've changed. I know." Dionysus spun around once to show off her physique. "Time and omnipotence will do that to a god. But enough talk. We leave now."

The Greek god-cum-goddess returned her gaze to me.

"As for this young intruder … let's just call it wrong place, wrong time."

She raised an arm above her head and pointed glowing fingers in my direction. Electrical charges filled the air. I shut my eyes.

The explosion was deafening. I nervously reopened my eyes. The charred remains of Judd Brown lay atop Dionysus. She pushed his corpse aside effortlessly. His body, now aflame, splintered and cracked. Dionysus rose from the floor and brushed ashy detritus from her slender arms and legs.

"He never was very smart," Dionysus said. She glanced at the smoldering walls. "The inferno is going to be spectacular …a fitting pyre for poor, sad Ampelos."

She pointed a finger in my direction. "Begone, child," she declared.

And I was.

———

I awoke late the next morning, certain that I'd been dreaming. But the smell of burnt wood and a glance out my bedroom window quickly proved otherwise. I raced to the kitchen. Mom and Dad were sipping coffee and sharing the morning newspaper.

"It lives," Dad said, smiling.

"Hey, what happened?" I asked, pointing in the direction of the old man's house.

"Yeah. The house caught fire in the middle of the night," Mom explained. "I'm surprised you slept through the noise and sirens."

"What about the old man?" I asked, already aware of the answer.

"Haven't heard," Dad said, "but I don't think the news will be good."

———

The Brown property has been vacant for many years. The hedge remains, and it's grown ridiculously high. Dad stopped trying to maintain it ages ago, long before the arthritis set in.

If there was an investigation into the cause of the fire, the results weren't released to the public. I'll never know why the old man sacrificed himself to save me. Maybe he was simply tired from 6,000 years of seclusion.

I often wonder, too, why Dionysus spared my life. Mythology depicts the Greek god as compassionate and benevolent. Perhaps she didn't want two dead bodies on her conscience.

Today I do what I can to express my gratitude: a backyard grape vine and a well-furnished basement wine cellar. Both symbolic gestures, I know, but the wine is good, and sleep has never been better.

Extra! Extra!

I THUMBED mindlessly through an old copy of the *Inquisitive Gazette* looking for my byline. Page 17:

Man Has Baby With Two-headed Sheep!

Such a horrible piece. I'd endured so much bullshit to snag the senior reporter position, but it still amazed me to read just how bad my stories were back then. Perhaps my stories were no better today, except that they were now written in the privacy of my own office. I sighed and pushed the issue away, nervously drumming my fingers against the desktop. I needed a lead, some action, and most of all, fresh meat. I was in a slump, and I knew it.

The phone rang, startling me to the point that I nearly knocked over the black coffee I'd purchased from the vending machine hours earlier.

"Mr. Slade?" a nervous male voice asked on the other end of the line.

"Yes." I didn't recognize the caller. "Do I know you?"

"No, I don't think so. But they're after me!"

Just what I needed: a loon on a lunch break. I decided to play along.

"Who are *they*?" I asked in the most serious voice I could muster.

"The gargoyles," he replied hastily, voice barely a whisper, as if revealing a dirty secret he suspected I already knew.

"Got a name, fellow?" I asked.

"Uh, I'd rather not say. They might hear me with their great pointy ears. And if they hear me, they'll find me."

"The gargoyles?" I asked with feigned concern.

"Yes, of course! Are you listening to me?" His voice rose in anger.

My tolerance was fading fast. "Look, buddy, tell me what you want or I'm gonna have to hang up on you."

"No! Please—hear me out, Slade. I think I can give you a real story here. Unless you'd rather I go to the *Examiner* instead?"

I gritted my teeth at the mention of our crosstown competition. "No, we can do this your way. Why don't you start at the beginning?"

"No. Not like this. As I said, they're listening right now!" His voice teetered on the edge of panic.

"Oh yeah," I replied, "with their great big pointy ears."

"And pointy wings, and toes," he added, as if we were a duo in a psychotic sing-along.

"What do you suggest we do?" I asked casually, hoping my practical question would calm his nerves.

"Meet me in person. Corner of Twelfth and E Street. Bring a camera. I promise you a photo of a gargoyle! Please hurry!"

The dial tone that followed was almost soothing compared to the caller's frantic mutterings.

On another day I would have let it go, just another crazy seeking his fifteen minutes of fame. Today was different. I was going nuts in the office and needed an excuse to head out.

I grabbed my jacket and the keys to the company news van and then walked to the photography department in search of Conner. In addition to being the best photographer on staff, he owed me a favor.

—

Conner guided the van through the dirty, murky streets as we headed to the address I'd been given. *Why can't the crazies ever live in a nice upscale neighborhood?* I wondered.

"Slade, this guy is playing you," Conner said, breaking the silence.

I shrugged. "Probably, but I couldn't stand another minute in the office. Be honest—you're glad to escape, too."

Conner grinned. "Guilty as charged. At least I can smoke out here." As if to prove his point, Conner withdrew a Marlboro from a soft-pack in his shirt pocket and lit up.

"Just be ready with the camera," I reminded him. Conner grunted in mock confirmation, driving his point home that he didn't buy a lick of the caller's story.

For me, this was more than a simple impromptu field trip. Throughout my career I'd interviewed hundreds of people. I could tell truth from a lie better than a polygraph. There was a spark of authenticity in the caller's voice, and a level of intensity that can only be achieved by gifted actors, strung-out addicts, or the mortally afraid.

Not that I took the whole gargoyles story literally—no doubt they were in the caller's head and, in that sense, were real enough to him. I simply needed a snappy headline like "Mind Demons Invade the City—Are You Safe?" and it'd be bye-bye slump.

Conner pulled up alongside a row of rundown apartments and killed the engine. The corner of Twelfth and E Street looked like a typical low-income neighborhood, but with one interesting distinction: the rundown apartments here were adjacent to a series of stately, tall high-rises currently being used as government offices.

Conner collected his camera equipment and stepped out of the van. I double-checked the battery level on my digital recorder and followed..

"You get a description of this guy, or what?" The aggravation in Conner's voice was palpable. He tossed aside the remnants of his cigarette.

Before I could respond, a slight, nondescript man in a beige overcoat emerged from an alley between two buildings.

I was somewhat taken aback by the stranger's appearance. Having conducted countless interviews for the *Inquisitive Gazette*, those who resided downtown were typically either drunks or derelicts. In contrast, our mystery man appeared neat and somewhat refined, more like an accountant than a typical *Gazette* reader or contributor.

He looked past Connor and me, focusing his attention at the buildings across the street with great anxiety. I followed his gaze up the side of a gray stone building and soon realized the cause of the man's concern. Leering lewdly down at passersby, and perched forward on muscular haunches, stood a great stone gargoyle.

"Let's move inside," the man said quickly, and retreated into the alleyway.

Conner rolled his eyes and mouthed, "He's crazy," as we reluctantly followed the stranger.

—

The meeting place resembled an old warehouse or factory. A subterranean chill surrounded the air and an unidentifiable stink permeated the walls and floors. Conner issued fake gagging sounds as soon as we entered the place. I kicked backwards and nailed his shin.

"Shit!" he cried out in pain.

"What's wrong?" our strange host asked.

"It's nothing," I quickly interjected. "My associate here is slightly asthmatic."

"For the record, I don't like profanity, so please clean up your language. If your friend is referring to the odor, then he is quite perceptive. This was a meat-packing plant many years ago. Some smells never fade."

"Can we take some photos?" I asked.

"Help yourself."

I nodded to Conner and he unpacked his gear. Soon the intermittent bursts of light from the camera's flashbulb were adding a strobe effect to this already creepy place. Conner moved into another room and the effect became somewhat less disturbing.

"Mind that your friend doesn't wander too far."

"This isn't your property, is it?" I already knew the answer but wanted to see just how far off the boundary of sanity our host had jumped.

"No, it isn't. But it's an important place to all of us. A sort of safehouse."

I was missing good material here. "Do you mind I record this meeting?"

"Not at all. I would expect nothing less from a journalist such as yourself, Mr. Slade." The man stared directly at me as he spoke, sending a shiver through my spine. I could barely discern his pale blue eyes in the near-darkness.

I shook off my discomfort and switched on the recorder.

"You were saying, Mr.—?"

"Mr. X for now, please.".

"Of course. You referred to this building as a safe house. To protect you from gargoyles?"

"That's correct. There's something they don't like about this place. I believe it's the fact that so many beasts were slaughtered here, and they, in one form, are beasts themselves."

I suppressed a grin. This stuff would sell a lot of newspapers. "You said 'in one form.' Can the gargoyles assume multiple forms?"

"Of course. Their other form, the most common form from old Europe, is the stone gargoyle."

"Such as the stone gargoyles atop the buildings here, at the corner of Twelfth and E Street?"

Mr. X paused. His eyes were on me again, probing, searching. I could feel his stare in the close darkness, a darkness that reeked of things long dead. Finally, he responded.

"Yes, like the stone gargoyles on the buildings here."

"For our readers, why have you decided to share your story?" Inquiring minds, mine included, wanted dearly to know the answer to that one.

Mr. X inhaled deeply. After several long seconds he released the air between his teeth. For a moment he seemed to increase in size by the simple act of breathing, an illusion that was doubtless the play of shadows on the wall. It was clear that my question disturbed him. I waited patiently for a response.

"Mr. Slade, I've seen so many things. So many horrible things." His voice became soft and faint like a candle slowly burning out.

"Things the gargoyles have done?" I asked. The conversation was taking a turn I wasn't expecting—a turn I wasn't entirely comfortable with.

"I've seen things they have done and will continue to do. You think time is significant when measured against the slow blood of stone?" he growled angrily, pressing closer to me.

I instinctively stepped back and realized with no little discomfort that I was nowhere near an exit. *Where the hell was Conner, anyway? I wondered. Damn him and his lousy cigarettes.*

I forced myself to remain calm and finish the interview. "For our readers, can you describe what you've seen?"

"I've seen the inside of a news van, its interior soaked with the blood of a dying cameraman."

That was it. I found the exit and bolted out of the decrepit building and down the alley, slipping on trash and old newspapers. I stopped at the sidewalk.

One back door of the van was open. It squeaked eerily back and forth on its hinges in the wind. The door repeatedly knocked against a foot that hung at an awkward angle out of the back of the van. A red smear stained the van's bumper and the pavement.

Horribly, incredibly, I found myself gazing skyward to the gargoyle across the street. A maroon smear ran obscenely across its jaws and its stony clawed hands were stained red.

Before I could move or speak, a spear of pain struck my back and dug in. I spine went numb as I was pulled down and dragged back into the alley.

Foul breath spilled across the side of my face, reeking of rancid meat and the stench of centuries.

"Like I said, newsman, so many horrible things."

The Flight Dummy

SUDDENLY I was awake, and just as suddenly alone. I figured the passengers to the right of my aisle seat had gone to the bathroom, but when I looked around, every seat was empty.

We were still airborne—I could hear the steady hum of the jet's turbines carrying me deeper into the night sky. I pressed the call button, twice to be sure, but nobody came. A movie was running on the overhead monitors, providing a soft light source in the dim cabin. Stunned, I stood up and walked forward, grasping the seat tops as we hit turbulence.

I whipped back the curtain to the first-class cabin—empty. I stumbled forward to the door of the cockpit and rapped on it smartly. I felt incensed. The other passengers must have deplaned while I slept in my seat. Why hadn't anyone awakened me? Claire, my fiancée, must be irate. We were to meet at the Orange County Airport, and now I was airborne at 35,000 feet and 600 miles per hour. My frustration grew with every passing moment. I pounded my fists against the cockpit door.

"Open up, damn you! You've made a mistake!" I screeched.

No response.

I turned back around and was stunned to see a diminutive passenger seated in the first row of the cabin. Beyond the windows, flashes of lightning illuminated the clouds like silver blood veined through a storm god's black heart. In that moment I realized that the passenger was merely an old corn doll, looking tired and faded in its burlap skin. Its eyes were crimson X's, each stitched of thread. I made the obvious assumption that the doll had been mistakenly left behind by a child during deplaning.. Still, the placement of the doll was curious—perfectly seated as if positioned intentionally. And wouldn't, I wondered, the flight crew have noticed the abandoned doll and arranged for it to be taken to lost and found? I pondered over the mysterious artifact for a moment while it stared dumbly forward, head lolling softly on its bean-bag belly.

I heard a clank and rattle from the rear of the aircraft and walked back to investigate. A drink cart rolled back and forth in the aisle, its cache of bottles tapping against one another as it bumped against the nearby seats.

The noise was more than my nerves could handle at the moment so I pushed the cart firmly into the serving alcove. A new sound took its place: a random metallic *tink* like a quarter caught in a clothes dryer.

I rolled the cart back into the aisle and noticed a small hatch in the floor of the alcove. The lid, slightly ajar, was the source of the sound. I ripped open the hatch and spied the outlines of the luggage and bags beneath me. The moment I poked my head in to investigate, I was assaulted by the stench of rotten meat. I felt like diving for a vomit bag, but instead fished a key fob flashlight out of my pocket. I held my nose and hung over the edge once again as I thrust the tiny beam of light below me.

There were bodies down there among the cargo. Several feet from me the pilot lay sprawled over a large green duffel bag, his uniform bloodied by a thousand small cuts. His eyes were sewn shut with two X's of red thread. Nausea came fast, but I managed to grab a vomit from the nearest seat back before expunging the tasteless airline food I had eaten an hour earlier.

I staggered up, convinced that this madness was the work of the corn doll, for I could conceive of no other reason, however illogical or fantastic that could explain my current predicament. Intent on destroying the little demon, I tucked away the obvious question in the back of my mind, somewhere behind my rage: *Why was I spared?*

Suddenly, the pressure was released from the cabin, and I was pulled forward up the aisle as oxygen masks fell from storage compartments and hung like alien entrails. My inner ears erupted in pain from the abrupt loss of pressure; my left ear began to bleed.

I clawed my way into a row and sat down, quickly fastening the safety belt. Just ahead of me, the corn doll clutched onto the edge of the mid-section door, whipping madly in the wind. The doll waited until it was certain we had established eye contact; of this I am certain. It then issued a mock salute with one miniature arm and winked with one eye, the crimson X folding into a dash. The doll released itself, and tumbled end over end into the slipstream and the stars.

Numb and frightened by the bizarre events, I began to feel faint from lack of oxygen and quickly covered my nose and mouth with an oxygen mask. Although I was surrounded by air masks, I had no idea how long I could exist this way, or how the loss of cabin pressure would impact the plane. I pressed my hands against my ears to shut out the howling wind and closed my eyes, convinced that this was truly the end but afraid to witness my own demise.

Then magically, impossibly, the blistering wind ceased. The mid-section door had been firmly closed and locked down by some unseen force. The overhead monitors went black. Seconds later, a message appeared on the screens in large white letters:

YOUR PUNISHMENT IS TO DECIDE.

The message began to flash up and down across the monitors. *Who was behind this?* I wondered. *Am I already dead, and refusing to open my spirit to the afterlife?*

I dashed up the aisle to the first seat of the first-class cabin. The cockpit door was open, banging back and forth on its hinges. There was nobody inside. I'd expected as much, based on my earlier grisly discovery.

But what surprised me, however, were the two items left neatly on the corn doll's seat. The first was a manual containing landing instructions. The second was a bottle of cyanide.

For the Children

JACK RILEY was behind the wheel on the road again. Somewhere up ahead, creeping through the silent cornfields that lined the interstate, the mist was creeping toward another victim. Somewhere up ahead another child would die.

Unless Jack got there first.

Jack wasn't the hero type; he was merely an old man who had finally found the good within himself. It was strange when he thought about it. He was doing it for the children. The children, he smiled to himself, the children who called him Old Man Riley and heckled him from the street. Now, removed by so many miles from the bitter soul that had been Old Man Riley, Jack understood their taunts; even forgave them. After all, had he been anything but a bitter, old man? *Yes,* he thought grimly. *you've also been a bitter, old drunk.*

His sons and daughters had long since grown up and found their own way. Not long afterward, Jack's wife followed them, fed up with her husband's perpetual drinking. All gone, leaving behind a miserable, empty wretch. Old Man Riley, that's what they called him, and that's exactly what he had been.

But no more. Now he was hunting the mist. The mist had forced Jack to look in the mirror and truly see himself for the first time in decades—sunken, dull eyes, long wrinkles that marred his face like scars. His time was running out. But before he died, he meant to perform a final act of goodness. He would do it for the children.

Jack called it *the mist,* but could have easily called it by its truer name: evil. For that's what it was, no matter its shape or form. Perhaps it had risen from the spoiled land of uneasy graves. Jack didn't know, and he supposed it didn't matter. What mattered was that it was after the children.

Jack watched the flat, uneventful landscape of the Eastern Shore scroll by. He passed a deserted barn on his left, long since left to ivy and the elements. The sun was setting low in its twilight, spreading orange and rose-red fingers across the sky.

It's a sick sort of race, Jack thought, *and either way Jack Riley will lose. When the mist chooses its next child, it will swallow the young soul without pause. And when I find the mist, it will mark my end as well.*

It didn't bother Jack to think of his death. He had seen his share of evil, but the mist was different. It wasn't the evil of 'Nam, or the evil contained in a bottle that had the power to wreck a man's life. Those were intangible, unreachable evils. The mist was different, absolute. Not absolute body, but absolute hate.

Riley passed an open pit barbecue, and the familiar smells of barbecued chicken filled his head. Next there were small antique stores, and lonely shacks with their fronts covered with tires and hubcaps.

Jack couldn't shake the terrible images from his head—the young girl and her wide eyes, the mist and the way it took her for its own. Jack hadn't met the girl before, but he figured that prior to the mist's arrival, he had despised her just like he had all of the other neighborhood children.

He had been recovering from his late-afternoon stupor, and had seen the girl walking alone down the street from his high bedroom window. Most residents turned in early, and this night had been no exception. Not to say the town was dangerous. It was a small, tightly knit community, safe even for little girls who walked alone late at night. Jack had watched from his window with detached amusement, his head pounding like a sledgehammer, wishing the girl would skin her knee and go bawling home to her mother.

That's the type of person he had been.

Jack hadn't noticed the mist at first; it seemed as if a piece of the night itself had begun to wrap around the girl, stifling her screams like a dark mattress. Then, like the wind, it had gone, leaving the cold body of a little girl in its wake.

The mist swallowed souls; fed on them. And Jack meant to free them, the soul of that little girl and countless others.

Jack looked down at the dashboard. He was doing over eighty. He clicked on the radar detector and it beeped to life, eerily breaking the silence that had reigned over the car's interior.

Jack was still thirty miles out of Bridgeville, the place where he thought the mist would strike again. It liked small towns. Small town inhabitants stay young longer than their city-dwelling counterparts who grow up hard and fast. The mist could never draw sustenance from the city. It would starve as it haunted the dirty tenements looking for a child of pure innocence, one truly unmarked by the world's pain. Small town kids seldom talked of drugs or crime or vandalism. Instead, they walk to corner stores and buy sodas, trade baseball cards, run through fields, and play in streams. Theirs was a world both slow and sweet.

Perhaps they're right, thought Jack, as he sped toward his destination. *Perhaps I really did learn all I needed to know in kindergarten.* Such thoughts came freely now to Jack Riley. He was a different person now, a person who had learned to care. He had never felt so alive before, or so real, and he knew that every mile toward the mist was also another mile toward the boy who had been Jack Riley.

Night was beginning to fall, and he switched on the car's headlights. His only companion on the interstate was a pickup truck that soon became a speck in the distance. The darkness made him uneasy, and he floored the accelerator. Jack was still twenty miles out of Bridgeville, and had no idea of how quickly the mist could move. It could already be there.

Jack became mesmerized by the flat stretches of pavement. His mind reached back, back into long-forgotten recesses, back toward his youth.

Jack remembered tasting fear as a boy. When he was six, a neighbor of Jack's named Tim Wilson went mad one summer evening and butchered his family in their sleep. Wilson had then stepped out into his front yard and shot himself in the head with a revolver.

The news had shocked the town, but somehow that wasn't the worst of it. People could forget the flashing ambulance lights, perhaps even the body bags that were loaded into the back, two smaller than the rest. It was the empty house that kept one from forgetting.

Talk had arisen, as talk always does, about Wilson and his secret dealings with demons and the Devil. At the time, Jack had not understood that it had been little more than baseless speculation and empty words. He hadn't known that sometimes people like Tim Wilson go crazy and hurt their own all by themselves, without help from the Devil or his imps.

Jack and his friends had believed the house was haunted, possessed, or both. They imagined figures behind the shuttered windows, glowing eyes that followed them on their way to the bus stop.

Soon, they'd decided it was time to find out the truth. Jack had approached the house, jeered on by his friends who talked boldly but made sure to stay behind him. The porch boards had creaked, just the way they were supposed to when evil was afoot.

"C'mon guys, we can't do this," he'd stammered. "We're breaking the law. And what if it *is* haunted?"

"C'mon, Jack. Don't be a girl. Break the window, and we'll crawl through," Curt Jacobson had said roughly.

Jack had looked back at them doubtfully, seeing faces full of resolve, and under the pressure of their eyes he'd said, "Someone get me a stone."

The other kids had run back into the yard and found him a real chucker. It was heavy but well-shaped, solid in Jack's nervous palm. Jack heaved the rock and shattered the living room window. He'd looked back at the boys, and saw that their faces were filled with doubt, reluctant to enter now that the taboo act had been done.

"C'mon," said Jack, "let's hunt some ghosts!" Careful to avoid the remaining shards of glass on the window frame, Jack had reached in, unlatched the window, and pushed it open. He'd then climbed through, expecting the house to smell of evil, wolfbane, and blood.

Instead he'd been greeted by the stale, musty odor that accompanies abandoned houses over time. The other boys tumbled into the living room, and they'd all sat together for several moments in awestruck silence.

They'd been expecting doors to mysteriously open and close, shouts and low voices to resonate through the walls, perhaps even the sound of gunshots. Yet nothing unusual occurred, and so the boys had begun to ease up a bit, mouths grinning.

Billy Whittaker, Jack's best friend, said, "There ain't no ghosts in here. Let's go."

"Of course there are no ghosts in here," said Ray, one of the other boys. "They wouldn't be here in the living room. They have to be in the bedroom, where it happened."

"Where *what* happened?" Jack asked with uncertainty.

"Where they got shot, dummy."

Everyone seemed to blanch.

"All right, sissies. Since you won't go, I will," Billy Whittaker boldly announced. "Just stand guard here."

Billy rose and began to walk down the hall.

"Wait, Billy. I'll go with you," said Jack.

Billy looked back and nodded, and that nod had said . *Yeah, I knew you'd come, Jack. We're best buddies. We'll leave those wimps behind.*

They'd heard no voices or clanking chains, saw no walking corpses in the attic, and yet somehow this lack of horror had made it worse. It made their journey to the bedroom seem forbidden.

Finally they'd reached the bedroom door. They had seen the

newspaper photos, yet to be here, in front of the gate where death had once walked, was indescribable. Yet Billy didn't hesitate. He was a go-getter, the type of kid who was always picked to be on the team. Billy wasn't scared of anything.

"Ready?" asked Billy, smiling wryly.

"Yeah . . . I'm ready, Billy," Jack said softly. Deep inside he knew he wasn't ready, could never be ready for what was waiting beyond the door.

Billy had placed a hand on the doorknob. It all seemed to happen in slow motion. Finally the door opened, falling back silently. The boys were suddenly flush with fear. Muted sunlight fell through the half-curtained windows, and the room seemed too clean, too cold, too distant.

Billy pointed to the carpet. Jack knew what Billy was pointing at, and he tried not to look. Curiosity had driven Jack's eyes downward past Billy's outstretched finger, and there in the carpet, beneath the beige, was a darker stain.

A single shot exploded through the silent room and chaos erupted.

A mad, bumping scramble had echoed down the hall and out of the window. On the front lawn stood the other boys, doubled over with laughter. Jack noticed a cap gun in Rays' hand.

Somewhere along Route 404 between Georgetown and Bridgeville the swirl of police lights in the distance roused Jack from his reverie. As he drew closer, he saw three police cruisers and an ambulance parked in a grassy strip on the shoulder of the interstate. Paramedics were loading a body into the back of the ambulance. A small body.

Jack pulled over and stepped out of the station wagon. His eyes were hot, and he felt tears might come at any moment. He choked them back and approached one of the police officers.

"What's happened here?" Jack asked desperately.

"Kid fell off of his motorbike running an errand for his mom and broke his neck. It's a damn shame. He was a fine boy. Everybody knew him. "

"So, it was an accident?" asked Jack.

"Don't know what else to call it. The bike was upright and still running when we arrived, but the boy was already dead. The officer looked at Jack with concern. "Do you know the boy?"

"Yes," answered Jack solemnly, turning back to his car. "I know them all."

Jack sped away. He did not know if the mist would strike again tonight, but he couldn't help flooring the accelerator. Jack felt responsible for the dead child behind him; all he could think about was beating the mist to Bridgeville. He couldn't bear to lose another.

Jack breathed a sigh of relief when his headlights splashed over a road sign that read:

WELCOME TO BRIDGEVILLE
IF YOU LIVED HERE,
YOU WOULD BE HOME NOW!

The houses in the town were large and close to one another, giving the street a cozy, Norman Rockwell aura. Jack imagined that that neighbors here knew one another, and that here the American Dream actually worked. The streets were empty, and the streetlights provided an abundance of light, adding to the overall safe and comfortable atmosphere.

Jack turned onto Main Street and cruised around the square. It was so much like his own town had once been–a little league baseball , a local Dairy Queen that promised heaping chocolate and vanilla twist cones, a family-run corner drug store with hand-drawn advertisements in the windows. Jack felt immediately attached to this place. He longed to cry, to weep openly, not for the dead boy on the roadside or for the dead girl, but for himself and what now realized he had lost through the years, and for what he had found again.

Children weren't idiots, Jack knew. They saw how simple life could be, and the magic was their belief in it. Jack wanted to race up into the church's steeple, swing wildly from the bell ropes, wake the entire town, and scream, "I understand! I finally understand!"

Jack drove a while longer and soon arrived at a bed and breakfast just off Main Street. He parked the car and surveyed the stately dwelling before entering. He would have preferred a Motel 6 had one been available.

The foyer was heavy with tobacco smoke, and the man at the registration counter was seated at a desk with his back to Jack. Jack cleared his throat softly.

"Oh, hello." The man rose and opened a ledger at the counter.

"Reservation under Jack Riley," said Jack good-naturedly

"Of course. Mr. Riley. Would you care for a soda or bottle of water?"

Jack noticed the small glass door refrigerator next to the desk. Bottles of Budweiser stared back at him like jaded eyes, as if calling to him. *C'mon, Jack, you remember us, don't you? Let's go for a ride. We'll have a real fine time.*

Jack looked away quickly. Everything okay, Riley?"

"Yes, thank you. I think I'll pass on the beverage."

"No problem. Here's your key. Room 3. Top of the stairs."

In the background a radio buzzed and crackled, reminding Jack of the boy's accident on the motorbike. He began to climb the stairs, and the clerk called up to him. "Any luggage, Mr. Riley?"

"I'll grab it later," Jack said, and entered his room, locking the door behind him to shut out the memories.

—

Sleep had been uneasy and, as usual, filled with the same recurring nightmare in which a small child stared up at his window, eyes wide as saucers in supplication as the mist approached.

And then the real horror had arrived.

The thing that had been Jack had closed the blinds and poured another drink. Outside, he could hear the whispering, the girlish shriek, but he kept the blinds shut. His eyes were only for the bottle. The dream unfolded as if he were viewing it from the perspective of the man who was quickly becoming a boy named Jack, and it broke him down to see what he had been.

He awoke with a start and shook off the unsettling visions. It was already 10:00 a.m. Jack silently cursed himself for having overslept. After a quick shower he walked downstairs for coffee and breakfast. For a little while he allowed himself to enjoy the cozy atmosphere of the old house, fears and worries subsiding as he cradled a coffee mug and savored a warm pastry. He felt pleased to be here among simple small-town folk. Their good nature reaffirmed his purpose.

Jack left the guesthouse and walked down Main Street, content to feel the sun on his back as he became acquainted with the town. Bridgeville seemed like a place trapped in time, a place urban sprawl had carelessly forgotten in its relentless attempt to swallow the world Jack passed the Dairy Queen and spied a group of local kids. *If I can reach them, I can save them.*

Jack ordered a vanilla cone and sat next to the kids.

"Hey guys, how's it going?" he asked.

Three of the four boys laughed.

"What are you bothering a bunch of kids for, mister?" asked the tall, red-haired boy. "You some kind of freak?"

Jack was temporarily stunned, and for a moment the only sound was the slow whir and whine of the overhead fan. He hadn't expected this.

"Beat it," the red-haired kid grunted.

Jack evaluated the group. The red-haired boy was obviously their leader, either by age or size. Two of the boys looked between him and Jack, uncertain what to do. The fourth kid averted his eyes and stared down at his sneakers, which dangled several inches above the tiled floor.

Jack didn't want a confrontation, so after waiting a moment he stood up and left.

"Hey, mister!" Jack turned around. It was the quiet boy from the Dairy Queen. "Don't mind Kyle. He just likes to show off."

Jack smiled. "What's your name, son?"

"I'm Stevie Mills. What's yours?"

"Jack Riley. You can call me Jack.

"You're new to the neighborhood, Jack?"

"Yeah. It's a nice town. Stevie, aren't you worried about talking to a complete stranger?"

"Nah. You seem okay," Stevie said.

"So do you, Stevie."

Stevie walked alongside Jack and finished their ice cream cones.

"Tell me, Stevie, who is the most well-behaved kid around here?"

"I suppose it's me," said Stevie, obviously embarrassed.

"I'd like to ask you an … unusual question, Stevie, but I hope you'll answer truthfully."

"Sure, okay."

"Do you believe in monsters?"

"Yeah. I mean, I know I shouldn't. My dad tells me that I'll never grow up if I don't realize there's no such thing." Stevie lowered his voice. "But I'm sure one lives in my closet. Couple under the bed, too. How about you, Jack? Do you believe in monsters?"

Jack stopped in his tracks and knelt down. "Stevie, what would you do if I told you that a monster was coming here, to Bridgeville, just for you?"

"Gosh, I don't seem that important for a big 'ol monster to come just for me."

"It's a special monster. It's only interested in good kids, kids who are well-behaved."

"Oh," said Stevie, looking troubled. "That's not good. Can I stop it?"

"I think so, but you have to trust me. Can you meet me at the park at four o'clock?"

"Yeah, but I have to be home for dinner by five. Mom's making broccoli. Yech!"

Jack laughed. "Do you have a dog?"

"Yeah, a big one named Casey."

"Here's a tip: Wrap your broccoli inside your napkin, and then drop it on the floor. Casey will eat it."

"Wow, Jack! That's a great trick!" Stevie exclaimed.

"I'll see you in the park at four."

"Okay. I'll try to be there."

After a quick lunch Jack napped in in his room at the bed and breakfast. He woke refreshed at 3:50 PM and headed to the park.

Stevie was already there, creeping up on a squirrel with a cookie. He got within several feet before the animal scrambled away.

"Geez," Stevie complained, "why did he go?"

"Perhaps he had to go back to his girlfriend."

"Squirrels have girlfriends?"

"Yes, and moms and dads who make them eat acorns instead of broccoli," Jack answered.

"Yech!"

"Stevie, do you remember what I told you about the monster?"

"You mean the one that only chases after good kids?"

"Yes. I think he is coming here tonight."

"T-tonight?" Stevie stammered, fear glazing over his innocent features.

Jack knelt down and gripped the boy's shoulders. "Listen, Stevie. The monster wants you because you're good." He pointed to Stevie's head and then his heart. "Good in here, and in here."

Stevie stared back, uncomprehending. He jumped as something brushed against his leg. It was only a cat slinking by, holding the stiff body of a robin in its mouth.

Stevie looked away from the bird. "I don't want to die, mister."

"Listen, Stevie, I won't let you get hurt. But you have to listen to me."

Stevie looked hard at him.

"Tonight, you have to sneak out of your bedroom and come back to the park. You'll have to move quickly because the monster will be close behind you."

"Sneak out? My folks would kill me if they ever found out about it."

"It's the only way. Otherwise the monster will come for you while you're asleep. If you come here tonight, we can stop it. Understand?"

Stevie nodded. A cool breeze swept across the park, kicking up leaves in playful dervishes. The wind stirred Stevie's hair; he looked both terrified and lost in that moment. The cat dropped the bird on the ground and jumped into the underbrush to continue the hunt. Seconds later, the robin perked up and winged away in a rushed flutter.

"Can we really defeat it?" Stevie finally asked.

"We can defeat it, but only tonight, only together. Be here at 11:45 PM," Jack said.

"11:45," Stevie confirmed.

Jack nodded and walked away, confident he had Stevie's understanding and, more important, his promise. He knew Stevie wanted to know more, but Jack figured the less said, the better.

—

Jack waited alone in the darkened park. The deserted merry-go-round moaned softly on its axle as it turned in the cool breeze. Around him, Bridgeville's inhabitants slept. Jack suspected that somewhere the mist was creeping through the town's streets—hunting and probing, sinuous and alert.

Quick footfalls approached and a small, silhouetted shape burst through the trees.

"Jack! It's after me!"

"Stevie, step behind me!"

The boy complied, and a second later the mist entered the clearing. Cloud white and unbearably cold, a strange red light glowed in its center. It emitted a sound akin to a downed electrical wire.

"Jack, I'm scared!"

"I know. Just stay behind me," Jack warned.

The mist moved to Jack's left, its tendrils extending closer to Stevie. Jack stepped forward into the mist and spoke.

"I survived you. I skipped stones by the lake. I wasted hours lying in the grass watching the sky roll by. I ate ice cream, and caught frogs in the creek. I was the best kid there ever was. The *best*."

The mist paused, hovering above the earth and thriving with malevolence.

"Yeah, that's right. I was the best kid there ever was. Jack Riley. I never cursed or wore muddy shoes indoors. I went to church every Sunday. I respected my elders. Not because I had to, because I wanted to. Because I loved my parents, my friends, my town. That's what goodness is. Love."

The mist began to hum, and prismatic splinters of color cut through its interior.

"I swam in the lake by our house. I loved its water. I remember the taste of wild strawberries and blackberry pie. I remember playing catch with my dad in the backyard. I remember it all."

The mist moved forward with renewed determination.

"Stevie, get back."

"N-no. No way," he stammered, trying to be brave. Jack kicked backward, sending the boy sprawling.

Cold tendrils found Jack, and he felt a sensation like ice water run through his veins as the entity sought Jack's purity.

"C'mon! You want virtue? I've got it in here!" Jack screamed, as pushed a fist to his chest. "More than you can handle!"

The wind increased, causing the merry-go-round to spin and squeak. Stevie whimpered behind Jack.

Jack felt cold from head to toe, engulfed by the mist. His eyes were blinded by flashes of sharp color. Slowly, he felt his chest tighten and he strained to breathe.

"I won't let you do this! I won't," cried Stevie, running forward into the mist. "Stay away from him!"

The mist appeared agitated, and its hold was now an arctic vice around Jack's neck and chest. It wouldn't be long now.

"Jack! Give me your hand!"

Jack reached out, fingers stiff and frostbitten, for Stevie's hand. Finally, their hands met.

The mist's hold began to loosen as Jack could breathe once again.

"That's right. The two best kids in the world. You can't win," Jack rasped out through raw throat muscles.

Jack and Stevie advanced.

"Mist, mist, go away, come again some other day," Jack sang.

The mist retreated with each word, shrinking in on itself.

"Tip a canoe, and Tyler too!" chimed Stevie, and they both laughed heartily.

The mist retracted into a small intense ball and spun rapidly in midair. Suddenly, it became blindingly white, like a new star. With a soft pop, like a balloon bursting, it was gone, leaving only wisps of smoke that drifted across the playground and up into the night sky.

"Jingle bells, Batman smells—" sang Stevie.

"—Robin laid an egg," finished Jack.

It was so good to laugh, thought Jack, so good to laugh like a boy again.

The Watcher's Web

THOUGHTS TURNED slowly in Rizzo's mind as he watched the luminous hands of his watch move toward the appointed time. It was 2:10 AM. His small, supple form was covered in a black wetsuit which stuck heavily to his damp skin. He rested in a cross-legged position on a tree stand with the tools of his trade laid out before him. Among these were the climbing spikes he had used to attain his position and a loaded pistol. A long silencer was attached to the end of the pistol's barrel. In his arms he cradled a scoped crossbow which held a light, triple-pronged grappling hook in place of a quarrel. The grappling hook was attached to seventy feet of light rope.

A light breeze stirred the leaves and cooled Rizzo who sweated intolerably from the heat caused by the wetsuit's insulation. Rizzo hoped the wetsuit would protect him when he made his unorthodox entry into the museum.

Rizzo was a lifelong thief, and thievery was his mistress. From jawbreakers in candy stores and apples in corner markets, his road to criminal activity had been paved early in his youth. By the time he'd reached adolescence, stealing had become Rizzo's passion. Anything he deemed valuable, from radios and purses to skateboards and bicycles, were lessons in Rizzo's criminal education. By fifteen, he'd joined a car-stealing gang.

Now, ten years later, Rizzo was beginning to discover that he was too good at his profession. The feds were conducting a nationwide search for the Jinx diamonds he'd stolen from a hotel safe in Vegas. Rizzo had little choice but to split the haul into small parcels to be sold to different buyers across the country. He'd pull in enough dough to live comfortably for the rest of his life, but Rizzo had no intention of living comfortably. His goal was to be filthy rich. Which is why he now rested forty feet above ground in a sturdy oak tree next to the National Museum of Natural

History. An opportunity for financial advancement had recently presented itself, and Rizzo meant to take full advantage. *After all,* he thought, *it's the American way.*

The opportunity had manifest itself in the form of an exhibit entitled The Lost Treasures of Spain. Rizzo had been relaxing on the plush, carpeted floor of his apartment sipping a bottle of Molson Golden when he learned about the exhibit. He'd been watching the story of Rob Lowe's sex scandal on *A Current Affair* with great interest when the show broke for commercials. Rizzo had risen slowly, walked with some inebriation into the small kitchen area, and grabbed another Molson from the refrigerator. When he returned, the television screen was filled with images of gold coins and jewelry, and the pleasant voice of the narrator describing the exhibit and explaining that all of the pieces on display were recovered treasures from sunken Spanish galleons. Rizzo plopped down into an easy chair and his mischievous eyes had gleamed with ingenuity.

Rizzo had soon phoned the home of a Jarvis Hannigan, a wealthy collector in the Florida Keys. Rizzo had dealt with Hannigan before, and knew that he'd pay anyone who could expand his collection. Hannigan was the sort of man who paid handsomely for quality items and had no qualms about purchasing stolen goods.

As Rizzo expected, Hannigan was quite interested in the contents of the exhibit. He'd offered Rizzo $2 million for prespecified pieces. Rizzo had gladly accepted. Hannigan had conducted business with quiet discretion in the past. Rizzo hoped that for Hannigan's sake, he hadn't forgotten how the game was played.

Rizzo glanced down at his watch. 2:15 AM. Crime time. He confirmed that the grappling hook had twenty-five feet of cord free to fly. The remaining cord was attached firmly to the tree stand to remove any risk of it feeding out accidentally. Rizzo made a final check of the knot, stood up on the tree stand, and raised the crossbow to a firing position. Fifteen feet above his position a decorative gargoyle adorned the museum building. Rizzo got the lower part of the gargoyle's wing in his sights and fired. The hook landed in the crevice between the gargoyle's gently curved wing and the wall. Rizzo pulled on the cord to confirm the hold was stable. He straddled the tree stand, wrapped the cord around his waist several times, and leaned back with all of his weight.

Rizzo donned custom-made leather gripping gloves and tucked the pistol into a shoulder holster. He removed the auxiliary cord from the stand and let it fall to the ground. An amateur would have hesitated. If the grappling hook slipped or the rope broke, Rizzo would plunge forty feet onto a cement sidewalk, assuming he'd be lucky enough to hit the sidewalk. Hitting the grass could result in paralysis and a shattered skeleton. Rizzo had checked and rechecked his equipment, but had been no way to perform a real test.

"No guts, no glory," he muttered through clenched teeth.

Rizzo smiled fiendishly as he pushed himself off of the stand. He swung through the air with the fanatical face of a World War II kamikaze pilot, savoring the coolness the velocity provided.

He crashed through the window, rolled, and drew his pistol. Hearing or seeing nothing, Rizzo rose to his feet. He removed a silencer from a compartment on the shoulder holster and screwed it onto the pistol's muzzle.

Rizzo had landed at the entrance of the South American Hall. A small amount of light radiated from the display cases which ran down either side of the corridor. The glassy eyes of a stuffed doo-doo bird regarded him calmly from its throne of simulated guano. Rizzo felt like blowing the bird's head off but disregarded the impulse and instead slunk down the room silently.

Halfway through the South American Hall, Rizzo turned right into a small corridor which connected the hall to The Evolution of Man exhibit. The central air had been shut off for the night, and Rizzo sweated profusely in the wetsuit. He paused to pick assorted glass shards, none of which had injured him, out of the wetsuit. After removing the larger shards, he continued to the end of the corridor.

Rizzo turned the corner and stopped. Soft light emanated from the display case in the center of the room. Two skeletons wearing tattered fabric rested side by side within the diorama. This, however, wasn't why Rizzo had stopped. Something else was in the room. Something he had felt but not yet seen.

Rizzo wanted to avoid whatever it was that was causing him to shiver with fear. He sensed an evil presence—something wild, something potentially fatal. But he could no more avert his eyes than an alcoholic could discard a drink. He was drawn to it the way motorists are drawn to stare at car wrecks; an element of fascination accompanied Rizzo's fear.

The source of Rizzo's terror stood in the far end of the room. The outline in the doorway was instantly recognizable. The museum guard stared directly at Rizzo. A voice in Rizzo's head badgered him nervously. *That's a guard! Remember the good 'ol days when we used to shoot guards who got in our way? Remember?*

Rizzo had nearly forgotten the pistol which hung listlessly from the sweaty palm of his right hand, but the voice in his head snapped him back to reality. Two shots penetrated the guard's chest. Years of practice had made Rizzo an excellent marksman, and guard should have dropped. But he didn't. Nor did he cry out or show any indication of pain. It suddenly occurred to Rizzo that the guard hadn't even tried to avoid the shots.

Rizzo screamed in rage, and emptied the rest of the clip into the guard. A bullet ripped apart the guard's right cheek. Another struck his neck. For a moment all was still. It seemed to Rizzo that the two skeletons on display were akin to lovers drifting calmly through the dark tranquility of space.

The thing—for Rizzo no longer considered the guard a man, or human for that matter—
began to laugh a cold rumbling sound both primal and animalistic. For a moment, Rizzo stood frozen and thought that were a wolf capable of laughter, this was what it would sound like.

He dropped the pistol and ran.

Rizzo flew into the next room and carelessly struck the corner of a display case. He cried out in pain and was propelled toward the floor by momentum. He threw both hands outward and barely avoided hitting the floor with his face. Rizzo immediately scrambled to his feet. The heist was now an afterthought. For the first time in his life, Rizzo was afraid.

He had barely gone two steps before a vice-like grip grabbed his left arm and twisted it behind his back forcefully. His radius snapped. Rizzo was still screaming when the thing lifted him off the ground and threw him toward a wall several feet away. Rizzo impacted with tremendous force. The impact shattered his nasal bone. A crimson trail was painted on the wall as Rizzo slid down it.

Tears of pain, rage, and fear coursed freely down Rizzo's bloodied face. He collapsed. The wall he'd struck featured a mural depicting Aztecs in the process of trepanning a young warrior.

The ritual involved hammering a spike into the man's skull to release the demons that possessed his soul. Rizzo glanced at the mural and felt sick. He turned toward his attacker who stood calmly, several feet away. The thing had removed a flashlight from its gun belt and seemed to be waiting for … something.

"What are you! What kind of monster are you!" pleaded Rizzo between sobs.

The thing's heavy, black police shoes echoed loudly down the hall as it walked over and crouched beside Rizzo's battered form. It lifted the flashlight up below its chin and replied plainly, "I'm the night watchman."

Then it clicked on the flashlight and showed Rizzo what he was up against.

Rizzo looked up into what was basically a normal human face of milky complexion, but for the fact that half of it had been blown off. The thing threw its head back into another fit of raw, resonant laughter, revealing two fangs where the eye teeth should have been.

"My God, you're a vampire," whispered Rizzo in a subdued tone.

"Yes, but I am also the night watchman. Run along little mouse; I want to build an appetite before I feast," it said pompously.

I'll be damned if I'll be your feast. Rizzo tried to rise but collapsed when he put weight on his broken arm. With no little effort, he was able to stand by pushing upward with his legs and right arm, keeping the left side of his body against the wall for as long as his balance would allow. He was shivering uncontrollably in the sweaty wetsuit. He leaned against the wall to catch his breath as imaginary newspaper headlines such as "Cat Burglar Killed by Count" and "Heist Attempt Foiled by Prince of Darkness" flew through his head. *Christ, this is unreal.* Wildly, Rizzo sprinted off into the darkness.

Rizzo screamed as he ran, hoping to attract the attention of another museum guard. He reached the second floor rotunda and galloped down the stairway to his right. The ominous sound of the heavy police shoes were behind him. He hit the first floor and dashed into the first hall on his right: the Sea Life Hall.

In the dim light provided by the display cases Rizzo saw the outline of the ALVIN submarine which was suspended from the ceiling. The huge bulk hanging above and to the right of the submarine was a full-scale model of a blue whale. Its shadow spanned the entire right side of the room. Three polar bears stood like ghosts at the far end of the hall, their teeth long and horrible.

On the day Rizzo had checked out the security systems he'd stood next to a group of school children as they stared up into the whale's fiberglass underbelly. Their eyes had been wide with wonder, and at the time Rizzo felt slightly embarrassed by their reaction. Hadn't they known the model wasn't worth anything?

Rizzo controlled his fear and stopped running halfway through the hall. The hand of his uninjured arm held his nose to control the bleeding. *Where in the hell were they?.* Rizzo had disabled the alarms in the South American Hall and the Evolution of Man Hall, but he'd left the rest of the system intact. His movement through Sea Life should have been detected.

Finally Rizzo heard the sound he'd been longing to hear. The hiss and crackle of a walkie talkie broke the silence at the entrance to the hall.

"Omega Twelve, this is Omega Control. Several of the silent

alarms in Sea Life have been tripped. Please respond immediately."

A pleasant, confident voice replied. "This is Omega Twelve back, Control. I'm on my way." A figure wearing a guard's hat entered the hall and began to rush toward Rizzo. *Oh dear Jesus, let it not be him, oh please dear God let it not be that monster,* thought Rizzo crazily.

The voice cried out, "Put your arms up in the air! Move a muscle and I'll blow you away!" As the man drew closer Rizzo could see the drawn pistol. Rizzo threw his arms up, wincing in pain. *It is just a cop; oh, thank God, it's only a cop.*

The guard and Rizzo were nearly ten feet apart when the guard stopped walking. Rizzo was still unable to see his face in the darkness. A low, cold voice said, "You're really much too loud for a cat burglar. It's time you learned who's the cat and who's the mouse."

The guard fired a shot at Rizzo that tore through his right shoulder, sending white flares of pain through his shoulder blade. Rizzo screamed and stumbled backward into a display case. He leaned against it and stared into the lusterless eyes of a giant squid as the blood from the wound dripped onto the tempered glass surface.

"Kill me now. Please, just get it over with," whimpered Rizzo as fat droplets of blood smacked against the floor like a leaky faucet.

"Not quite yet," the watchman replied, "there is still the feast." He walked over to Rizzo who could feel its bated breath spill hotly over his neck. The watchman leaned down and licked the blood from the case's surface. His tongue danced with serpent speed across the glass. Rizzo was shocked to see that the watchman's damaged face had already begun to heal.

Without warning the watchman unzipped the neck of the wetsuit and plunged its fangs into Rizzo's neck. They felt like miniature daggers. Once more, tears coursed freely down Rizzo's face. He kicked and convulsed, but was able to offer limited resistance due to his broken arm and wounded shoulder. Soon Rizzo was still.

Rizzo's body knew it was dying. Endomorphins had been released, and his thoughts became hazy and dreamlike. He was barely aware that the thing in the guard's uniform had removed its fangs from his neck. It zipped up Rizzo's wetsuit and carried him over to a bench in front of a viewing monitor. The thing hit the switch on the back of the unit. To Rizzo it seemed to be speaking like a record album spun in reverse .

"I thought you might enjoy some educational TV while you died. Don't worry, this won't take but a second. I'll hit you right between the eyes. It'll look as though I missed once and took you out with a second shot. The police might have some questions about the broken arm, but who's going to take me to court for killing a cat burglar?"

The meaningless sounds confused Rizzo. He turned his attention to the TV where a ridiculous-looking walrus with glasses appeared on the screen and said proudly, "I am a walrus. I belong to a family of mammals known as pinnipeds. Literally translated, pinniped means 'fin-footed.' The word is derived from the Latin root *pinni*, meaning fin, and *ped*, meaning foot…" Rizzo looked away from the monitor to the blurry, blue creature beside him.

"You don't know this, but the flesh of vampires regenerates. My face should be completely healed within a few minutes, after which I'll walk to the locker room and change into a clean shirt. I've brought your pistol from upstairs. I assume you know that vampires can't be killed with standard bullets. I was careful to handle it with a cloth napkin so it only has your fingerprints. The pistol will be placed in your hand. The whole clean-up process shouldn't take more than seven or eight minutes, which is good because by that time the control room will start getting worried and dispatch officers up here.

"When I'm finished I'll return here and await their arrival. I'll leave my radio here so Control can't detect that I've left the Sea Life Hall. Then I'll tell them how I shot a cat burglar sneaking through Sea Life. I'll explain that I had no way of knowing the thief's pistol was empty when he took aim at me. They'll say I did the right thing and it's a damn shame he's dead but it wasn't my fault and I really should go home and sleep because the cops will take care of it from here. Yeah, that's the standard response. I know because I've done this before. Not here, of course. I'm not foolish.

"Over the centuries I've been the night watchman at warehouses, loading docks, and of course, other museums. Always there, always watching, always waiting—waiting for someone like you to come along and provide me with a little entertainment, nourishment, and moral justification."

Rizzo turned his attention back to the screen. He now saw real walruses, thousands of them, lounging on slabs of white ice in a blue, Arctic sea. Suddenly one of the walruses that was acting as lookout started barking madly, and on the edge of the screen appeared the black fin of a killer whale knifing through the water toward the unsuspecting mammals.

"Stand up! It won't look good if I shoot you while you're sitting down."

Rizzo was confused for a moment but understood when the thing in the blue shirt tried to pull him to his feet. He stood up and turned his attention back to the walruses.

Now Rizzo saw his face on the lookout walrus, and as he barked madly for his friends to flee from the sleek black and white killer, he began to understand why they paid no heed to his cries.

He was its prey.

Rizzo rolled clumsily off the ice and into the freezing water. He swam fluidly and efficiently, but as he looked back the whale was closing the distance between them. It had opened its terrible mouth revealing rows of knife-edged teeth. Panicked, Rizzo swim even faster, but as he turned around a second time, the whale bit fiercely into his neck.

"Don't worry, I never miss," said the watchman as he pulled the trigger.

Rizzo saw the whale swim away with the walrus in its mouth. Blood flowed from the walrus's neck and made dark clouds in the water. Soon the clouds dissipated, leaving nothing behind but the cold, blue expanse.

Dreaming, The Copper City

CARTER LOOKED out over the dry sea. Shuttlecraft flitted about the lunar sky like fireflies.

There were a thousand life domes beneath his own, and thousands more beneath the Moon's surface.

Carter's mood was bitter. *Man finally lived on the Moon, and for what? There was no attempt to elevate the race, no attempt at Grecian grandeur or Egyptian magnificence. Just more of the same—exploit, exploit, exploit—until this planet, too, became a mined-out husk like Earth.*

To divert himself from his own negative thoughts, Carter pondered his plans for the evening. He glanced at the Virtual in the corner. The gloves and helmet hung on the wall like a puppet under construction. *No, not again tonight.* Carter always felt dirty after a session of VR eroticism, and his sessions were becoming way too frequent.

Carter turned his attention back to the observation window to pursue his favorite hobby: dreaming.

In the lonely hours by the window Carter had observed many phenomena—solar flares, comets, shooting stars—but always from the safe distance of hundreds of thousands of light years. Tonight was different.

The object was large, its size an obvious measure of its proximity to the Moon's surface. But there was no doubt it was large. And falling fast.

It landed in a remote area of the colony, a flashing streak over the life dome clusters announcing its arrival, then nothing more. Had he blinked, Carter would have missed it.

But Carter hadn't blinked. And he didn't plan on missing it.

—

Carter switched the APCC Terrain Rover to off-road mode and turned off the paved lane which led away from the colony. He'd traced the meteor's path and knew roughly where to begin his search. Soon the distant lights of the life domes that comprised the colony were only as dim as the stars themselves.

Carter was lulled by the electric hum of the Rover's life-support system as it carried him over the lunar surface. He rode without audio, preferring to dwell in silence on the mysterious emotion propelling him toward the alien rock.

After ten minutes of sleepy, uneventful travel Carter spotted the meteorite. It had embedded itself into the rock just before the geography fell away into the massive depression of what the colonists called "The Big Empty." It emanated a pulsating green glow.

Words suddenly formed in the even hiss of Carter's oxygen intake: *"Yog Sothooth! Shigguth! Yog Sothooth!"* Carter ran a diagnostic on the life-support equipment and double checked his radio. Everything seemed to be in order. He attributed the audio hallucination to his trance-like state of mind.

Carter reached the impact site, donned his helmet in a nanosecond, and raced toward the broken object. There was nothing exotic about the stone's exterior, but the piece that had broken away revealed a pulsing green liquid trickling out from the core.

Was it radioactive? Carter couldn't be sure. If the authorities knew that he had been inspecting the meteorite he'd face weeks in quarantine. *But they would not know.* He felt unnerved by this thought and the one that followed: *But they must not know.*

As he knelt down to better inspect the object, Carter noticed diamond-like crystals floating within the emerald liquid. He placed his hand on the rock, an incredibly stupid action, but his will overcame all reason.

The instant the insulated glove met the rough surface, Carter's soul left the Moon…

He spun through a vortex of color and speed where all sense of time and location were lost to him. Images appeared, so dim and murky that they were more like impressions— amorphous, reptilian creatures moving about in a deep abyss. He felt revulsion at these sensations.

But there was also great joy and beauty as he captured impressions of a slight, golden-skinned race of humanoids playing, loving, and teaching…

Unconsciously, Carter removed his hand from the meteorite, and his soul returned to the Moon.

He steadied himself as his vision came back into focus. For a moment he felt as if he might vomit, which could have proven lethal in his suit, but he forced the warm bile back down his throat.

The lights of a colony patrol appeared in the distance. Carter gathered up the meteorite fragment and sprinted back to the Rover.

Not bothering to remove his helmet, Carter closed the hatch, switched off the safety lights, and sped around the lip of The Big Empty, avoiding the direct route home.

—

Carter revealed his obsession with the stone to no one. His physical appearance soon became deplorable. His stringy dark hair grew down to his shoulders and his jumpsuit reeked with a myriad of odors. His boss notified HR, and the colony psychologist was sent to interview him. Carter always managed to avoid the visits by telling one lie or another.

The stone was a gateway to a copper city—*the* Copper City— into which Carter now constantly projected himself, a realm to a far-away world that he would depart only to meet his body's urgings for sustenance and sleep.

He would sit for hours, dreaming languidly with a poet's far-off stare, clutching the chunk of stone in his lap which enabled him to tread the copper suspended walkways of the golden creatures' city and glide through crystal buildings that defied all human architecture and measurement.

More and more often, there were the darker times—times when Carter clutched the stone dripping with sweat as he observed black, slimy, bulbous masses oozing around in the sewers beneath the Copper City and the black-bearded acolytes that called them forth from the darkness with a thunderous chant: *"Yog Sothooth! Shigguth! Yog Sothooth!"*

One day—Carter couldn't be sure of the specific date; as the days now seemed to blend together—Carter understood the message of the dark priests as clearly as if their mantra had been uttered in English:

The centuries of tranquility for the nonbelievers above ends with our march. The double suns, Auspus and Syrus, will sear your flesh when you break the earth— let the pain strengthen the fury of our attack!

(THE BLACK BEASTS BEGAN TO THRASH IN THE DARKNESS)

Beauty shall be replaced with one being: Yog Sothooth. The New Arts will portray one image: that of the one true Lord, Yog Sothooth. We will live with divine purpose: to serve our Lord, Yog Sothooth, and his dark concubine, Shigguth.

When his voice commands us from his undying grave beyond the stars, we will march. We shall surge forth from the sewers as one body and smash the city above and make sacrifices of its citizens. We will make monuments to our Lord, a palace for his blessed homecoming from his starry prison.

There was no more, only the unholy grunts and liquid sounds of the black army moving about among the network of sewers.

Carter set the stone down. He was filled with great urgency. Strangely, he had grown to love the Copper City and its inhabitants more than he loved the Moon colony or the very Earth itself.

He took a deep breath and brought the stone up once again. Carter doubled his efforts to reach the populace of the Copper City, but the citizens went about their cycle of studying, conversing, and painting, unknowing and unhearing the voice of their alien benefactor.

Carter made up his mind. He would have to reach the Copper City in person lest a race thousands of light years away would be annihilated, a race that could elevate all of humanity to higher purpose.

—

Carter hid within the cramped confines of the food processing unit of Exploration Shuttle R5-21A, bound for Jupiter. It was a risky hideout. If the food processer was fired up, he'd likely be burned alive. But it wouldn't be long before crew hibernation commenced, so he figured there'd be no food preparation on the trip.

A slice of the meteor rested above his heart in a vest pocket of his spacesuit, and at present he was unable to project himself to the Copper City. He had not been able to project through his suit since the day he'd first placed a hand on the meteorite.

Carter only needed the crew until the craft was synchronized with its preprogrammed flight path. So he suffered through the g-forces of liftoff and the ensuing escape from the Moon's gravitational pull.

Finally, after what seemed like days, but had only been the better part of two hours, the shuttle broke away from the moon and the crew left their liftoff stations to resume normal in-flight duties. Like all colonists, Carter was familiar with shuttle flight operations as the commerce between Earth, the colonies, and the Moon employed all but the highest administrative and security personnel.

After leaving the liftoff stations, a series of checks and tests would be run including diagnostics analysis, flight path confirmation, engine output assessment, hull stability, and life support systems validation. However, on small exploration shuttles these tests were typically performed remotely from the flight control center team who would transmit a report to the shuttle crew. This was precisely why Carter had opted to stow away on an exploration craft. The crew was minimal, and their activities before entering the hibernation chambers were nil.

After reviewing the uploaded report from the control center, a final assessment of the life support systems was done, after which the majority of the crew went into suspended animation. One crew member was assigned to "watch the stars go by" while the others slept. This protocol existed mostly to avoid corporate liability for any accidents that might occur during the flight. Shifts ran for two years on average.

Shuttle R5-21A had been assigned a crew of three—two scientists and an engineer. By accessing the ship's schedule from the computer link in his life dome, Carter had discovered that the engineer was scheduled to take the first shift while the scientists slept in the hibernation chambers. Carter had also been able to circumvent the security modules and retrieve the access codes required to operate the Planet Rover, which was stored in the shuttle's cargo bay.

Carter couldn't recall when he'd stopped loving and caring for his neighbors and coworkers. He only knew that somewhere on the streets of the Copper City they had ceased to be a concern. It was only that beautiful, scholarly race of golden people who waited innocently for its destruction that interested him.

Somewhere along the way he felt that he'd become comfortable with killing his own kind. Carter suspected this was true as he twisted the engineer's neck until it snapped and he shoved the corpse out of the pilot's chair. He confirmed its truth as he studied the faces of the two scientists—angelic beneath the soft glow provided by the coffin-like hibernation chambers—and removed their oxygen cables. Their life forces hissed away into the eternal silence of space.

Carter sat in the pilot's chair alone upon the shuttle. He removed the piece of the meteorite from his breast pocket, and projected himself to the sewers beneath the Copper City…

The invasion was close at hand. The dark priests poured over the astral charts, waiting for the dark solstice that would herald their master's homecoming.

There were thousands of the slithering, oily creatures now. And what terrified Carter the most was not their number but the fact that they oozed forward in clearly delineated rows and columns…

Feeling a tightening in his chest, Carter dropped the stone and waited for his heart to slow.

That last projection had literally sucked away his life. Clumps of hair fell from his head like black down feathers. His deep-set eyes were pink and red from swollen and broken blood vessels. Carter donned globes and placed the stone atop of the navigational computer. Somehow he knew it would guide the craft to the Copper City.

Ironically, Carter ate a ham sandwich from the food processing unit before entering the suspended animation pod.

—

Red pinpoints of light pierced Carter's eyelids and woke him up from the dreamless sleep.

He climbed groggily out of the hibernation chamber and studied the onscreen images being projected from the shuttlecraft's external cameras. Not only had the stone guided the craft to the alien planet, it had also enabled the ship to travel at warp speed and successfully initiated the landing sequence.

Carter was dismayed by what he saw. Unlike the turquoise sky which provided the harmonious background for the minarets and suspended walkways of the Copper City, visibility was limited to only a few feet beyond the shuttlecraft due to the violent winds which ripped apart the shifting sands.

He was nearly moved to tears. *Had he arrived too late? Had the downward spiral that he'd begun light years away on the Earth's moon yielded nothing more than a dead planet?*

But Carter did not cry. He fixed a cup of coffee from the food processing unit and readied the Planet Rover for operation.

—

The Planet Rover screamed through the desert at 300 miles per hour. Powerful streams of pressurized air shot out from the Rover at all sides, pushing back the swirling sand and providing limited visibility for thirty feet in every direction. Carter set the Rover for travel within a large particle stream and mesh shields dropped over the air intakes to prevent sand from entering the engine.

Two sensor bots ripped through the air in front of the Rover at 500 miles per hour; their aerial cameras provided Carter with constant feedback of the terrain ahead.

The cameras revealed a large structure directly ahead, and Carter ordered the sensor bots to zoom in on and hover over the structure.

Although distorted by sand, it seemed to be an artificially constructed mountain.

Upon reaching its base, Carter saw the mass for what it was: a mound of rubble.

Carter donned the helmet of his special environment suit and began to climb the jagged, irregular stones, the sensor bots whirling feverishly above and feeding images back to his handheld imaging device. He found strange objects among the fallen stones: coins, tablets, shards of pottery.

He had nearly fallen backward twice and was tiring of the climb when he received a new image: a black pyramid structure at the summit. While still trying to concentrate on the placement of each step, Carter nonetheless doubled the speed of his ascent.

At last he pulled himself over the small ledge which was the foundation of the black pyramid. The structure was perfect in every dimension, and was coated with an unnatural sheen which gave one the impression that water was constantly flowing down its sides.

"Yog Sothooth" had been scrawled in white chalk on the ledge in front of the pyramid, but something else captured Carter's attention.

Atop the pyramid, a silky garment of the type worn by the inhabitants of the Copper City fluttered insanely in the vicious wind like a diseased flag. . It had been fouled with blood and a black-green noxious substance.

The obsidian eyes of the pyramid sprang open, invisible to Carter. It studied him for a second with its cold stare, then it ripped free from its foundation, scattering Carter and the rest of the rubble that had been the Copper City across the planet's surface.

"Yog Sothooth..." shrieked the wind, and the dream of the Copper City died with it.

The Huntress

SAMUEL GRAY studied the dripping wax of the candle as it burned low. The hour was late, and little sound reached his loft high above the Baltimore Harbor. He loved this time of night, for only late in the evening would the harbor winds fully blow away the smell of the fish markets on the street below.

Samuel was the grandson of the late Dorian Gray, that unfortunate soul bound precariously to his own portrait. While the lavish lifestyle of his grandfather was not present, the love of art was readily evident. Paintings covered every wall, from floor to ceiling, and stacks of canvases leaned all about his large wooden desk, as if somehow additional wall space would soon appear from the ether. Even a casual observer would have realized Samuel was not just an art collector, but a painter in his own right.

Although his years numbered only thirty, he carried the demeanor of a much older man, and this impression was reinforced by his reclusive nature. While gambling and drink consumed many of his peers, Samuel was content to simply study his collection of artwork until the small hours of the morning.

It was during one of these reflective moments that the accident happened. It would have been considered a minor event had it not altered the course of all that would follow. Samuel had fallen asleep at his desk slightly past 3 AM. His elbow slid across the surface of the desk, tipping over an open can of red paint. The paint traveled across the surface of the desk and dropped from its edge in a slow, steady stream, making impact with a canvas leaning against the table leg.

With a gasp of dismay Samuel awoke, grabbed the canvas, and threw it onto the desk to review the damage. He hadn't had the opportunity to review this particular painting before, and was struck by its raw beauty. The piece, rendered in acrylic, depicted a woman atop a white horse and was called "The Huntress." She wore a silver crown adorned with leaves and rode sidesaddle on the horse as she blew into a golden hunting horn. Samuel studied her green eyes, red hair, and pale skin.

A streak of red paint flowed diagonally from the base of the canvas across the horse and the figure. The painting was effectively ruined.

"Don't fret," a voice called from across the room.

Samuel bolted to his feet, knocking over his chair in the process. The woman from the portrait was reclining on his bed. He rubbed his tired, bloodshot eyes, certain he was dreaming. But she remained present.

"About the painting, I mean," she continued. "Don't fret. You have set me free."

"Are you real or am I mad?" he asked.

The woman laughed, the sound like tiny bells chiming. "I am one reality, just as I was another, separate reality during my time frozen within the portrait. Now, let me paint you."

"Me? There's nothing special about me at all. I'm simply a self-taught artist, nothing more."

"Must I persuade you?" she asked, rising as softly as mist from the bed. She stepped toward him, her forest green tunic rustling like the breeze from the open window. She walked around Samuel's desk, knelt, and pressed her lips to his. Her breath was like autumn leaves and moss, and her lips like fresh strawberries.

He felt dizzy, and she laughed again. Her laugh seemed to descend from all of the cherubim in heaven itself. She took his hand and guided him to the bed. Laying him down, she whispered softly in his ear in an ancient tongue while stroking his brow. Samuel swore he heard the night music of crickets and toads in the distance, but he suspected his senses deceived him. He was wonderfully sleepy.

Hastily pushing aside Samuel's sundry belongings, the lady moved toward an easel, canvas, and paints at the front of the bed. She hummed a strange sing-song tune as she worked. Although Samuel tried to protest, to put an end to this foolishness, but his limbs were heavy and noncooperative.

"I'll soon be done," she promised.

—

Later that night, no one noticed the pale lady in the green tunic as she quietly slipped away from Samuel's apartment and disappeared into the harbor docks. Several days later, having received no word from Samuel, a family member insisted the police break down his apartment door.

Samuel was gone, but there was a new portrait on the wall. In this portrait a man with Samuel's likeness sat at a desk staring with a haunted expression at a picture of a white horse.

The Faerie Lights

REST AWHILE, friend, for it is clear that you have walked far over hill and valley, and penetrated the wild and strange woods, to have happened upon this corked bottle and its long-preserved manuscript beneath the moss-covered rocks.

I came upon this very spot, perhaps many years ago now, as just a lad. Here I took my respite, beckoned by a fair breeze sweeping over the verdant fields and a song sung in dulcet tones far sweeter than any produced by mortal throats. I was weary from hiking many miles, and my body eagerly fell into a deep sleep.

A song floated over my consciousness, sung by a thousand childlike voices:

> *Weary traveler,*
> *Rest your head,*
> *And sleep awhile*
> *Where the faeries tread.*
>
> *Weary traveler,*
> *Laugh in kind,*
> *And take deep draughts*
> *Of faerie wine.*
>
> *Weary traveler,*
> *Spend the night,*
> *Follow the trail*
> *Of the faerie lights!*

Something awoke me with a start, and I was astonished to find myself surrounded by scores of tiny, ethereal beings with Elvin features, swaying joyfully through the air on gossamer wings as they laughed and sang.

They brought the tiniest of goblets to my parched lips, and from the cups flowed the most intoxicating wine made of clove and dandelion. I noticed then that the sun was falling. Dozens of tiny hands tugged me to my feet. The faeries beckoned for me to follow. My journey was dreamlike, as I was under the spell of their golden drink. They began to glow like will-o'-the-wisps as darkness descended over the landscape.

Finally the small shapes converged in a dark, eldritch wood full of black, stunted, and gnarled trees. I felt compelled to follow, and though I was scratched and my garments ripped by errant branches and thorns, the magical wine had numbed me to all pain.

Finally I followed them into an entrance carved into a hillside. A moment later, however, I tripped over a root and tumbled down into darkness. I knocked my head and was soon unconsciousness.

I awoke to a jovial ruckus, or so I thought. The same beings alighted around my head and, upon seeing me awaken, rushed forward with hollow acorn husks brimming with fluid. In the near-darkness, I assumed that it was more flower wine, but the drink was thick, with a bitter, coppery taste.

As I turned to spit out the foul fluid, I found myself restrained by hundreds of silklike threads. It was then that a wind swept into the wretched hollow from outside, stirring the embers of a fire in the center of the room. In that brief moment I saw that the features of the faeries had changed; what had previously appeared light and airy had become dark and sadistic.

They wore coats of opaque mail, and their eyes, once innocent and wondrous, had become hateful yellow slits. They waved wicked, curved blades like those wielded by the Turks.

But the second accursed wind brought darker tidings and visions than the first, for when it swept the chamber and sparked the fire, the purpose of this dark gathering became all too clear. Tiny incisions had been made across my ribs, and many a faerie dined on bloody strips of pink meat skewed on the ends of their evil blades.

I know not what strength of God allowed me to break free of my bonds, swat and smash away those little demons, and haul myself out of that pit-like burrow into the cool night air, but I did not rest in my flight until reaching this very spot, where I recovered my wits and breath on these very rocks. It was here that I rested and recorded my tale for you, the unwary who follow in my footsteps.

So, weary traveler, do not tarry long in these unhallowed woods. Leave before the night arrives, lest you too fall victim to the faerie lights.

The October Man

MELINDA SITS in a rocking chair on her front porch, gently swaying back and forth. She rests her hands across her full, pregnant belly.

Her small farmhouse is along the Washington and Old Dominion Trail in Leesburg, Virginia, and even the yuppies that had invaded the small town of Leesburg so many years ago are asleep now, leaving Melinda alone with her thoughts.

The moon hangs fat and full overhead, and it occurs to Melinda that midnight is approaching on this Halloween night.

With a reluctant sigh Melinda rises from the chair and picks up the shovel leaning against the front of the house. She isn't looking forward to the labor of digging a hole in the hard Virginia red clay.

She realizes it was on a night like this, many years ago, that she first met The October Man. Melinda swings the shovel over her shoulder and walks down the porch steps as she recalls that strange encounter in these very woods.

She was younger then, and although she did not care for most of the changes brought about by the rapid population and housing growth in Leesburg and neighboring Ashburn, Melinda approved of the well-maintained Washington & Old Dominion Trail that spanned many miles to points east and west.

The Luck Stone rock quarry also bordered the trail, and although the daily explosions were annoying, the quarry soon became a long-term fixture and part of Melinda's personal landscape.

The park service installed a bench overlooking the quarry, and after long walks Melinda liked to rest there and watch the dump trucks crawling up the quarry road, weighed down with stone, so far away they resembled Tonka trucks.

One day at twilight after walking later than usual, she sat down to rest on the bench. As she started scanning the quarry, Melinda thought she saw two luminous green points of light floating in the water, but figured it was just a trick of the fading light.

Something softly touched her shoulder, no harder than a falling leaf. Melinda turned and was shocked to find a man standing next to the bench.

"I'm sorry! I didn't mean to startle you, Miss," he said, in a very proper English that didn't match his youthful appearance.

"May I sit down next to you?" the stranger asked, and Melinda found herself nodding and blushing all at once.

The time that followed was a blur. Melinda wishes she could have savored every delicious moment, but somehow time had accelerated to the point where she felt she could only be a witness rather than a participant.

There was talk, so much talk that the moon eventually rose high above them in the sky. Watching outside of herself, Melinda felt embarrassed by her endless giddy chatter, but seemed unable to stop it.

And the man seemed to listen.

Not just listen, but sympathize in a way that men rarely do, as if he truly understood her. Soon their talk progressed into handholding, and then into kissing.

Only while kissing him did a moment of discomfort, even fear, come over Melinda. At first she welcomed their embrace; his tongue seemed to tickle the back of her throat with its probing. But it quickly felt forced, like a vine or tube penetrating her esophagus, and as she began to push away the sensation of asphyxiation passed.

Melinda was pleased to continue holding hands with the handsome stranger after their passion had slowed.

Suddenly the man cocked his head and looked at the moon. He then glanced at the quarry, as if an unknown signal had caught his attention.

"Goodnight, Melinda, I will see you again soon," he said, kissing her hand.

Then he was gone. Startled, she stood up, but could not see him walking away in either direction. Fearing the worst, Melinda ran to the edge of the cliff overlooking the quarry, but saw only a dense fog drifting over the quarry's dark waters.

Suddenly Melinda was overcome by a wave of guilt. Her father, who was extremely sick, counted on Melinda every evening for prayers. Although her father had a dedicated hospice aide, she knew he would be anxious until she arrived home.

She quickly started down the Washington & Old Dominion Trail toward home. Melinda had no idea of the time, but by the height of the moon overhead she could tell the hour was growing late.

Her romantic evening with the stranger seemed like a dream. *Had it even happened at all?* Melinda touched her right shoulder where the man had clasped her strongly during their kiss. She gasped in pain when she ran her fingers over a bruise that had begun to form.

It was real!

Elated, Melinda almost ran home. She felt like her heart itself was a balloon that, if not tethered to her body, would soar to the very moon itself.

Melinda reached the farmhouse and stepped inside, quietly closing the door behind her. She crept up the old stairs quietly and was relieved to see her father resting comfortably. His hospice aide, Imagene, was dozing in a chair at Dad's bedside.

That night Melinda enjoyed a deep, restful sleep. She dreamt of being romanced by the handsome stranger on a magnificent homestead and having many children.

The next day Melinda woke up early, energized by the promise of a new day. She hummed as she made coffee, and sang and skipped as she fed the chickens and performed other chores. Her happiness was sweet and filling, and it welled up from a place from deep inside Melinda that had been dormant for a long time.

Imagene entered the kitchen and found Melinda dancing in front of the stove while cooking eggs.

"Good morning, Imagene! How's Dad?" Melinda asked.

"He's his usual grumpy self," Imagene replied, and they shared a heartfelt laugh.

"Well, you're certainly in a good mood today," Imagine observed. "Is the young man anyone I know?"

"What do you mean?" Melinda asked, blushing but trying to act serious.

"C'mon, Melinda. I haven't always been an old hospice nurse. Once upon a time I was young and carefree, even beautiful according to some men. And you know Reggie and I were married for years."

"I know," Melinda replied. "I guess I'm busted! But please don't tell Dad. Anyway, I don't think you know him. I barely do myself."

"Does your mystery man have a name?"

"Of course he does! It's just that … well, it's just that I can t recall it.

Imagene looked at Melinda with her mouth agape. "Well, aren t you something! Just be careful, Melinda. Love can be a dangerous thing."

Melinda nodded. She smelled something burning.

"The eggs!" She exclaimed, and rushed back to the stove.

The afternoon dragged on forever. Melinda and her mysterious man preferred the twilight hours since there were fewer joggers and cyclists crowding the trail.

Melinda had nothing to do but wait. She swept the porch several times, and even started counting the airplanes coming and going from the nearby Dulles International Airport.

Finally, the sun began to set, and it was time to make her way to the quarry. Imagene's words kept coming back to her: *love can be a dangerous thing.*

She wished Imagene hadn't said that, and she tried to forget about it as she walked.

The trees whispered in the breeze and the powerlines in the distance hummed. She was disappointed to find the park bench deserted.

She bit her lip trying to hold back tears and sat. She had worn a special sundress for him. It was lighter than the others, and goosebumps sprouted up on her bare arms from the cool breeze. An hour passed. Melinda was about to leave when she felt the light touch on her shoulder once again.

"Hello? Is anyone there?" she asked, anxiously looking around.

No one answered.

"Stupid girl!" she scolded herself. "Of course he's not coming back for you!"

Melinda shot off the bench and stormed down the trail toward home, tears coursing freely down her face. Once home she ran upstairs.

"Melinda?" her father rasped from his bedroom. "Melinda, what's wrong? Why were you out past dark?"

"It's nothing Papa ... I'm ... I'm fine. We just needed some milk." Melinda walked to her room and closed the door, eager to be alone as she cried herself to sleep.

That night she dreamt that a plant had taken root inside of her. Roots and vines pushed outward from her belly, covering and squeezing her insides until they felt as if they would burst. Tiny thorns scraped against her womb like a pumpkin being cleaned of its pulp.

She bolted upright in her bed, covered in a cold sweat, feeling crampy and clutching her abdomen, still shaking from the nightmare.

She wished she had never met the man by the quarry who had made her dare to feel desirable and pretty.

As the days wore on Melinda became somber and despondent. Her stomach cramps became more frequent, and to her astonishment her stomach had developed a small but noticeable bump.

She tried to put on a good face around Imagene and her father. She wore loose-fitting clothes to mask the swell in her belly.

One day sitting outside on the porch in her rocker, Imagene confronted Melinda.

"Are you going to tell your father, child?" She asked firmly but with sympathetic eyes.

"Tell him what?" Melinda challenged, all the while knowing fully her meaning.

"You can't fool me, Melinda. First you go on about meeting this exciting young man, and then you're with child!"

"I am not pregnant!" Melinda retorted.

Imagene quietly took a seat in the empty rocking chair next to Melinda and clasped Melinda's hands.

"Melinda, honey, I understand. When I was young, I had an unwanted baby as well. There are options."

Melinda broke down into tears. "You don't understand! We only kissed! I swear I don't know what's happening to me!"

Imagene shook her head and held Melinda. The two rocked in silence until Melinda's sobs subsided.

—

On the night before Halloween Melinda awoke from a nightmare. In the dream she had brought fresh flowers into her father's room on a bright and sunny morning while he slept soundly. She'd placed them on the windowsill. He'd sat up suddenly in his hospital bed and pointed a bony hand at her in accusation. His eyes remained closed as he'd uttered a single word: "Whore!"

During last week Melinda had felt energized and alive, in touch with all of her senses and the natural world around her. She had heard of this phase of pregnancy where the body suddenly realized it was hosting a second living being and kicked into overdrive to meet the new demands placed upon it.

With her senses heightened, Melinda was spending more and more time on the front porch in her rocker. It also helped her avoid to Imagene. Although Imagene had not disclosed Melinda's secret, it was clear to Melinda that Imagene didn't believe her. Imagene had begun pestering her to see a doctor to check up on the baby.

The wind blew across the porch, sending dried leaves scraping against the old floorboards. A voice in the wind prickled the small hairs on the back of Melinda's neck. It called out to her: "Melinda, come to the quarry."

She sat up in the rocker and listened again. Perhaps the stress was getting to her.

But the voice came again, beckoning her.

It had to be him. She had given up on romantic fantasies weeks ago, and now just wanted answers about what was happening to her body.

Pushing up with both arms, she slowly managed to raise herself from the chair. Her round belly made even the most basic motions difficult.

Melinda knew it was a bad idea to march out on Halloween night in her condition, but she couldn't resist the voice that continued to beckon her.

She made the trek down the path to the quarry. The voice grew stronger with each forward step.

Before lowering herself on to the bench, Melinda looked out over the dark waters and saw two glowing green points of light in the fog. They swirled above the water's surface.

It's him.

She waited while the fog rose and spilled over the edge of the cliff, filling the small clearing. The haze dispersed, reveling a figure in its midst.

The stranger strode toward Melinda and knelt before her. He placed her hands in his own.

Melinda wanted to slap him but instead squeezed his hands upon gazing into his compassionate eyes.

"Where have you been?" she asked desperately.

"Down there," he replied. "Beneath the waters of the quarry."

"But ... how?" Melinda asked.

He rose and sat down beside Melinda.

"I'm sorry, Melinda. I have much to tell you. My name is Paul Stafford. I lived near here long ago—160 years in fact, back during the Civil War. I was part of a Confederate unit, and as the war turned against the South the Union Army reached Virginia. We tried to hold them off near the Sully Plantation and they broke through. Those of us left alive scattered to save our families. I returned home to Emily, my pregnant wife."

Melinda listened in disbelief.

"We held each other until we could see the fires of their torches, then ran here to the quarry and threw ourselves off the cliff rather than fall into their hands."

"This is all utter nonsense," Melinda said. "I won't be conned."

"I know it sounds extraordinary, but every word I've said is true. Search your heart and tell me if you believe otherwise."

After a moment, Melinda spoke in earnest. "I'm so sorry."

"Thank you, Melinda."

"I've problems of my own, you know." She gazed downward at her swollen belly. "How did this happen?" she implored.

"My death was … unusual," Paul explained. "Perhaps it was the ancient waters of the quarry in which I drowned, or the power of these woods. I don't know for certain. But every October I'm allowed to come back, to walk among the living."

"When I saw you that first night on the bench, you reminded me of my Emily. She was as beautiful as you. It was, I admit, selfish of me to approach you, but I've been alone for so long."

"It's okay. I wanted it too!" Melinda exclaimed.

"You don't understand, Melinda. My seed is passed not through natural fertilization, but by the sharing of a deep kiss. This is why you are pregnant today. But my seed is cursed, not unlike the quarry waters."

"This is no curse," Melinda said, rubbing her stomach. It's a blessing! Our child will be born into this world!" Melinda exclaimed, leaning over to embrace Paul.

He abruptly pushed her away. "You don't understand!" he stormed, rising. "I'm sorry I did this to you, Melinda. But tonight you will lose the baby. And every subsequent October you will become impregnated, and on every Halloween night that pregnancy will be lost."

"You bastard! You're sick; demented! Why would you make such a horrible claim?" Melinda cried out.

"Because it's true. I'm sorry, Melinda," Paul said as he faded, retreating into the quarry in a cloud of mist.

Melinda felt an intense cramping in her stomach and fell onto one knee in front of the bench. Warm blood began to flow down her thighs.

She screamed in agony as the baby began to come out of her.

Then the cramps stopped.

Trembling, Melinda stared down in horror at the stillborn infant, a malformed, lifeless being no larger than a baby chick.

Sobbing, Melinda tore away a piece of her sundress and carried her baby home. She arrived shortly after midnight. The moon was full and golden overhead, providing ample light.

Wanting not to disturb her father or Imagene, Melinda quietly bathed herself from water she pumped from the well. She then found a shovel in the barn.

She treated the bundle carrying her baby lovingly. "It's ok, honey. It will be all right," she told it soothingly. Determined to keep her secret safe, she walked back to the trail, cupping her baby in one arm and carrying the shovel in the other.

Many Octobers passed.

Melinda's father died during the winter following that first October, and Imagene found work in a nearby nursing home.

Melinda's neighbors regarded her as kind but reclusive, and the land developers who approached her about selling the farm were politely turned away.

To her relief, Melinda never saw Paul again. He had given her enough. He had given her his gift, and she loved nothing than more to rock on her front porch, gazing at the October sunsets and massaging a full, round belly.

She was now an old woman but was still able to make the trek to visit her children when the weather was good. Past the powerlines she had discovered an isolated clearing in the woods, and there her children waited, aligned in a neat, well-maintained little row. During her visits she would typically sit atop the ground before their graves and tell them about Paul, their father, and hum nursery rhymes to them.

Sometimes a mysterious mist would appear and dance around the clearing as Melinda sang to the children. The powerlines hummed along in the distance, and life was good.

ABOUT THE AUTHOR

R. DAVID FULCHER is an author of horror, science fiction, fantasy, and poetry. Major literary influences include H.P. Lovecraft, Dean Koontz, Edgar Allen Poe, Fritz Lieber, and Stephen King. He is the author of several collections including *The Lighthouse at Montauk Point and Other Stories*. In 2024, David's weird fiction stories will be collected in *Asteroid 6 and Other Tales of Cosmic Horror* (Gravelight). His work can also be found in the anthologies *Hard-Boiled and Loaded with Sin* (Hawkshaw), *Halloween Party 2019* (Devil's Party), and *Halloween Party '21* (Gravelight).

More at rdavidfulcher.com

ASTEROID 6
AND OTHER TALES OF COSMIC HORROR

R. DAVID FULCHER